The Gold Cross of Killadoo

The Gold Cross of Killadoo

John Quinn

Children's
POOLBEG

To Derry, in whose kitchen much of this book was written, and with acknowledgement to Dr Pat Wallace, Director of the National Museum, for the inspiration of his writings and broadcasts on Viking Dublin.

First published 1992 by
Poolbeg Press Ltd
Knocksedan House,
Swords, Co Dublin, Ireland

© John Quinn, 1992

The moral right of the author has been asserted.

Poolbeg Press receives assistance from
The Arts Council / An Chomhairle Ealaíon, Ireland.

ISBN 1 85371 220 5

A catalogue record for this book is available from the British Library.

Cover design by Judith O'Dwyer
Set by Richard Parfrey in ITC Stone Serif 10/14
Printed by The Guernsey Press Company Ltd,
Vale, Guernsey, Channel Islands

Contents

1

The Raid

Eoin was out of breath. He flopped down in the tall grass and rolled over on his back. "Wait!" he called. "Wait, Derval!" He panted out his sister's name and spread his arms in the waving grass. They had been running for what seemed like hours and he was exhausted.

"Eoin! Eoin, we have no time for games. Where are you?" His sister's voice was urgent and bossy. Eoin smiled to himself. He hadn't intended this to be a game but he enjoyed teasing Derval. He lay still and said nothing. "Eoin! If you don't answer me, I'll just leave you to the boars and the—"

"All right! I'm coming! I'm coming!" Eoin jumped to his feet. "I knew that would scare you!" It was Derval's turn to tease now. She laughed and tossed her long fair hair from her shoulders.

"I wasn't scared!"

"Were so!"

"Wasn't. I was just resting. It's a very warm day to be running like this for—for half the day!"

"Half the day indeed! We only left home a little while ago. You're just lazy—and too fat!" She poked a finger playfully at her brother's chubby arm.

"Am not!" he said, throwing a wisp of grass in her face. "Anyway, I don't see what all the hurry is about. We have all day to get to the monastery."

"No we haven't! And that's why! Listen!" Across the fields there came the sound of a bell pealing urgently. "The monks are being called to prayer! Now will you get up and hurry?" Derval ordered impatiently.

"Oh all right. I'm coming. We'll be in plenty of time. That's Brother Fergal ringing the bell. He always rings it early for the brothers who are working in the field."

"Well, even so. I want to be in good time to see the gold cross. Brother Killian promised us it would be finished today, so—what is it now, Eoin?" Her brother was not listening to her. He was staring at the woods in the distance. "Eoin!"

"What? Oh sorry. I thought I saw people moving through the woods just now."

"It was probably Aengus the woodcutter."

"No, there were several people there."

"Well, who could it be then?"

"Don't know. Norsemen, maybe?" He gave a nervous laugh.

"Don't be silly, Eoin. The Norsemen have never come this far." "Not yet!" Eoin watched the expression on his sister's face darken. He jumped up. "Anyway—let's go and see the cross. Race you to the round tower! Yayyy!"

"That's not fair. I wasn't ready!"

Eoin was already weaving his way through the tall grass before Derval made a start, but she soon made up the lost ground. She was two years older than her brother and her long legs took far fewer strides to cover the short distance to the tower. She gave a triumphant shout as she brushed past her brother. She heard him call out in pain but she didn't stop. He wasn't going to trick her twice. Their shouts and whoops echoed across the fields.

□

At last the great tower of Killadoo loomed before them. Derval scrambled over the boundary wall and staggered up to the base of the tower. "There! I win! I win!" She had scarcely enough breath to announce her victory. Eoin half-fell over the wall and collapsed at his sister's feet.

"Only—" He fought for his breath. "Only because you tripped me!"

"Did not. You fell yourself!"

"Did so!"

"Did not. Anyway it serves you right! You cheated at the start!"

"No I didn't. I said—"

"Come, you two! Do you ever stop arguing?" The tubby figure of Brother Killian loomed above them, his moon-face beaming a warm smile down on the embarrassed pair. Derval struggled to her feet.

"Oh, hello, Brother Killian. We—We've come to see the cross."

"Oh, indeed, " Killian giggled. "I knew you were coming this last while! I could hear the shouting across the fields!"

Derval ignored the monk's remarks. "Is it ready? Is it finished? Is it?"

"Patience, my friends! Patience!" Killian placed a hand on each head.

"But we came especially to see the cross," Eoin pleaded.

"And so you shall!"

"So it *is* finished," Derval gave a little leap of joy. "Oh come on, Brother Killian. Where is it?"

"You don't expect me to carry a gold cross in my habit, do you?"

"Well, where is it then?" Derval stamped her foot in annoyance.

"Really, Derval. You are a most impatient girl!"

Derval looked away quickly. "Well—we've come a long way," she whispered.

"All right! All right! I've been too hard on you!" Killian put his arms around both children. "I'll take you to Brother Cormac. He's polishing the cross before we place it in the oratory. But first..."

"Ah Brother Killian," the children chorused.

Killian ignored them. "But first...a present for your mother. I promised her something in return for the broth she sent me last winter when I was not well."

"Yes, Brother," Derval sighed, "but the cross..."

The monk turned to the boy and stopped. "Eoin, you have my sympathy. How do you put up with this girl?" he asked with a wink.

Eoin took the hint. "Oh, it's a hard life all right!"

Derval muttered fiercely to herself. Killian gave a hearty laugh, his belly heaving beneath his habit. "Ah, poor Derval. We tease you too much! Come!" Brother Killian led the children down a narrow path into a quiet corner of the settlement. He paused near a group of little mounds and held up his hand. "Listen! Our friends the bees are busy at work!" The air was heavy with the humming of bees. "The little bees; they work so hard and then give us the fruits of their work!" Derval was beginning to lose her patience again when Killian reached into the long grass and offered her something wrapped in cloth. "Here! A fine pot of honey for your mother. Mind you don't spill it!"

"Mmm!" Eoin mumbled. "My teeth are watering already."

"Thanks, Brother Killian," Derval said. "Our mother will be very pleased. Now can we see—?"

"Shhh!" Eoin interrupted his sister. "What's that noise?" The three froze and listened intently.

"It's just the bees, silly," Derval said.

"No, child. Listen!" Brother Killian put his hand on the girl's shoulder.

"It's...It's horses," Eoin cried, "and men...running."

"You're right, child," Killian said with anxiety. "We have visitors! Run, let you! Run! To the tower!"

"Who? What visitors?" Derval was bewildered by the sudden change in the monk's voice.

"Norsemen! Run!" Killian barked.

"But what about you?" Eoin pleaded.

"I'm going to hide the gold cross. That's the sort of thing these 'visitors' are interested in. Now go!" Killian pushed the two children in the direction of the tower and, leaving the path, he waded through the long grass towards the chapel.

"No, we'll help you," Derval said defiantly. "They'll never suspect us."

"And anyway, we came to see the cross," Eoin added.

"Stupid children. Don't you realise your lives are in danger?" Killian pleaded. "These Norsemen ask no questions. They'll..."

"They'll have to catch us first!" Derval laughed, but a bit nervously. "We're coming with you, Brother."

"Oh all right!" Killian shook his head in desperation. "If the Norsemen don't kill me, your mother will! Come. We must hurry."

The children followed as Killian waddled towards the

little church. Behind them the noise grew louder and warning shouts pierced the air as other monks realised the danger. The bell began to ring again—far more urgently this time. "Cormac! Cormac! Come quickly. We must hide the cross!" Killian shouted as he burst into the church. It was so dark inside that even with the door open it took a little while for the children to get used to the absence of light. Eventually they were able to distinguish a bent figure huddled before the altar. "Poor old Cormac!" Killian muttered. "Too busy to hear anything!" Cormac was humming away to himself as he polished.

Even in the poor light the brilliant sheen of the cross took the children's breath away.

"It's so beautiful!" Derval sighed.

"Well we haven't time to stand and admire it now," Killian urged. "Come, Cormac. We have visitors—the Norsemen. We must go to the tower."

The old monk clasped the cross to his chest and muttered in whispers.

"Wait!" Eoin cried. "Look, Brother Killian. You take Brother Cormac to the tower and we'll make a run for it with the cross!"

"With the cross? You?" Killian's round red face looked as if it would explode.

"Of course!" Derval chirped. "The Norsemen won't bother with us. We'll wrap the cross in this old cloth and I'll hide it in my cloak."

"I don't know," Killian shook his head. "If anything happened to you—or the cross..." He watched Cormac shuffle slowly away. "But then, we might not make it to the tower.." He scratched his head. "All right! I'll take the chance."

Eoin and Derval looked at each other in anticipation.

Killian had to wrestle with the old monk as he prised the cross from his grasp while trying to explain his action at the same time. "Here!" He handed the cross to Derval. The look on his face showed that he still was not sure he was doing the right thing.

"Be careful! Go back through the bee-garden. Run! God protect you! God protect all of us. Go!" He turned to Cormac, who stood at the door of the church with a puzzled look on his face. The children ran away through the tall grass.

"Come, Cormac," Killian cried. "I don't think either of us would be able for those Norsemen. We must get to the tower!"

2

One-Eyed Leif

The invaders had by now swarmed into the monks' settlement. They wasted no time, dashing in and out of the monks' cells, grabbing what seemed useful or precious. A group of them worked their way through the little church, stuffing whatever valuables they could find into their tunics. The air was filled with the cries of the Norsemen and the frightened squeals of the animals that were being rounded up.

In the middle of all the confusion stood one man. He was very tall, towering above his fellow warriors. A thick furry animal-hide was draped around his broad shoulders and added to his immense size. His wild mane of fair hair almost matched the colour of his bright yellow tunic. He stood, legs apart, leaning on a huge sword, surveying the destruction all around him. Even more striking than his huge size and his garish clothes was a great black leather patch that covered his left eye and half of the left side of his face.

As he watched his men, a greedy smile crept across his face. "Quickly, men!" he roared. "Fill your sacks with everything precious you can find! I want no rubbish! Only the best will do!" His great voice boomed across the settlement. "Hurry now! A flask of wine for the man who finds the most valuable piece of gold or silver! And look!" His great sword flashed in the sunlight as he swept it up to point to an enclosure on his right, "those pigs! They will feed plenty at my wedding feast! Let's have them too!" He gave a great laugh that echoed above all the din.

Brother Killian gave an anxious glance over his shoulder on his way up the ladder of the tower. He gripped the ladder even more tightly. Anger welled up in him as he saw what the Norsemen were doing. He felt like going back down and taking them on with his bare fists but he knew that was silly. Safety was the most important thing now. Above him, old Brother Cormac struggled and puffed. "These old bones of mine are creaking, Killian," he panted. "I don't think I can go any further."

"Come on, Cormac," Killian coaxed, trying to remain calm. "Just another few steps and we're safe!"

"Climbing ladders at my age," panted Cormac, "is not my idea of fun."

Killian looked anxiously over his shoulder again. "And being run through with a Norseman's sword isn't mine! Come on now, Cormac." His voice grew more urgent. "Here we are—just one more step. There! That's it! Safe at last!" He called out to another of the monks who cowered in the darkness. "We're the last! Haul up that ladder quickly or we'll have the Norsemen joining us in the tower!"

An arm reached out of the dark, grabbed the ladder and began hauling it through the doorway. Old Cormac knelt down and peered out. "Oh! Such destruction! Why must they wreck everything? Why don't they just take what they want and leave?"

Killian crouched above the old man's head and viewed

the confusion below. "I've heard these Norsemen are pretty thorough when they come visiting!" he said. "See that giant of a man with the beard and the eye-patch? That must be their leader, Leif leath-shúil! The one-eyed Leif! I've heard stories about him!"

Cormac strained his eyes to follow the direction of Killian's outstretched arm, which pointed to the giant below. The smoke that drifted across the settlement from a large fire beside the oratory almost obscured his view. Suddenly the loud squealing of frightened pigs pierced the air.

"Our pigs! Our pigs! They're taking our pigs, the—the—the pigs!" Cormac struggled to his feet, knocking over Killian, who was crouched above him. "Give me that ladder!" the old man cried. "I'm going back down to talk to that one-eyed savage!"

"No, Cormac, no!" Killian gripped the old man's shoulder firmly. "No one talks to Leif! You'd end up just like the pigs—with your throat cut!" He looked back at the other monks and barked an order. "Get that door closed, quickly! Do you want a Norseman's torch tossed in here to keep you warm?"

His sharp words brought immediate action. Figures moved out of the shadows and slowly a great heavy door slid across the opening. Cormac, on his knees again, followed the door and peered through the smoke. "My beautiful pigs!" he cried. "I've fed them since they were babies! Grrr! Bad cess to you, Norseman!" he roared at the giant figure below. "I hope someone pokes your other eye out!"

Leif was unlikely to have heard Cormac's angry words, such was the din all around him. Pigs squealed unceasingly as they were packed into a cart, while near Leif, the Norse warriors tossed the ornaments they had gathered into another cart. "There, Leif! Not a bad day's work eh?" one of the warriors shouted as he held a book-shrine aloft for his leader to admire.

Leif inspected the cart as further spoils were thrown into it. "Bah! I've seen better, Toren." He picked up a candlestick, examined it and threw it back into the cart. "There's nothing outstanding in this lot. Only a week to go to my wedding and I still have not found a gift for my bride, my beautiful Helga. What on earth will I do?"

Toren tried to be helpful. "You could give her those fine pigs, Leif." The smile slipped from Toren's face very quickly as he felt the might of Leif's right hand smash into his jaw. He reeled backwards under the blow.

Leif's one eye blazed with rage. "Don't insult my beautiful Helga," he roared. "She shall have those pigs all right—but only for our wedding feast—a feast the like of which Dyfflin has never seen! You understand?" He towered above the fallen Toren.

"Yes, Leif," Toren muttered.

The mood of the one-eyed giant changed once again and he burst into laughter. "Hah, Toren! You are a stupid old ox but you're a good warrior and you're still my friend, even if you do insult my Helga!" The other warriors, who had been watching nervously, joined in their leader's laughter as he offered a hand to his fallen friend—the same hand that had felled the luckless Toren. "Come!" Leif barked. "It's late and we must get to Dyfflin before dark. It's…"

"Leif, listen!" Toren pointed towards the bee-garden. "Something moved over there!"

"Oh it did, did it?" Leif whispered. "Well, let's meet that something!" He gave a full-throated roar and charged into the bee-garden. "Yahhh! Come out of there, miserable monk or I'll slice you in two." His voice dropped suddenly when he found himself facing two children. "Well—what have we here?" he called in surprise.

"S-stay away from us, you big—bully," Derval stammered, trying to sound unafraid.

"Hah! What's this, Toren? A young nun—and a spirited one at that!"

"I'm not a nun!" Derval was angry now. "We're only visiting the monastery. We are the children of Diarmuid, who is a cousin of Maolseachlainn."

"Maolseachlainn! I've heard of him. He's king of these parts." Leif's pretended fear amused his warriors.

"Yes," Eoin butted in, "and if you harm us, you'll feel the sharpness of his sword!"

"Hah!" Leif leaped back as if terrified. "I like this pair, Toren. Maybe we should bring them with us to Dyfflin."

"You will not!" Derval said defiantly as she backed away.

"Who is to stop me, little girl?" Leif noticed Derval's awkward movement. "Tell me—what have you got behind your back?"

"It's nothing. Just—just something for my mother."

"Well, let's see it, my little one."

"I'm not your little one—and if you want it, here it is!" She had taken the cover off the honey-pot behind her back and in a flash she splashed the honey right into Leif's face.

"Aargh!" Leif spluttered as he tried to claw the sticky mess from his eye and beard. His warriors giggled and sniggered. He turned on them. "Who dares laugh at Leif? If I see a smiling face I'll slice it in two!" There was immediate silence. Leif turned back to Derval. "As for you, you little vixen, I'll teach you to make a laugh of Leif! Come here!"

"Run, Derval, run!" Eoin cried.

Derval turned to escape but Toren had already blocked her route. He grabbed her cloak roughly. A little bundle wrapped in cloth fell to the ground. "Well, what have we here?" Toren asked. "Another present for your mother?"

"No! No!" Derval screamed. "You can't take that!"

"Oh yes I can—and I have!" Toren laughed as he opened the bundle with great curiosity. When the glint of gold caught his eye he gave a low whistle of surprise and called his leader.

Leif was still having difficulty clearing the mess from his face. "Stupid children!" he muttered. "What is it now, Toren?"

Toren slowly drew the gold cross from its wrapping. "What about this for your bride's wedding?" He tossed the cross to Leif.

"You have said it, Toren!" Leif smiled through the mess on his face. "This is what I've been waiting for. What a beautiful brooch this will make for Helga—or a neckpiece, maybe—when I melt it down."

Derval struggled to get free of Toren's grip. "You can't do that!" she cried. "It took the monks a year to make it— and it's a holy cross. God will punish you for it."

"Quiet, brat!" Leif roared. "Nobody punishes Leif! And my god is gold!" His lips curled in an evil smile.

"Don't forget the flask of wine you promised," Toren reminded him.

"You shall have it, my friend, and welcome!" Leif said softly as he turned the cross over and over in his huge hand. "At last—a fitting wedding gift for my beautiful Helga!"

3

The Gold Cross

Derval grew more and more angry as she watched Leif
twirl the gold cross around in his huge hand. The honey
had seeped through his beard and was dripping down his
tunic. "Great hairy beast!" Derval thought. "Who would
want to marry a monster like that?" She turned to Eoin.
Something had to be done to prevent Leif from taking the
cross. The buzzing behind her gave her an idea.

"Eoin!" she whispered. "The bees! The bees!"

Eoin shrugged his shoulders in puzzlement.

"What? What's that?" Leif snapped. "What are you
two up to?" He became aware of the dripping honey
again. "What a mess this stuff is!"

Derval tried again. "The bees, Eoin," she whispered.
"Release the bees."

Leif grew more suspicious. "What are you saying, girl?"
He grabbed her arm roughly.

"N-n-nothing!"

"Maybe I can persuade you to tell the truth, then!" he
snarled as he twisted her arm viciously.

"Let me go. All right! All right! I'll tell you." She
pointed to the nearest beehive. "There's more gold—lots
of it—in there!"

"What? In that little box?"

"Y-yes!"

His greed got the better of Leif. He bent down and peered into the beehive. "It's dark in there. I can't see anything."

"Take a closer look, you great big...pig stealer!" Derval shouted, giving Leif the mightiest shove she could manage. Normally her tiny frame would have had no effect on Leif's great bulk but here Derval had the element of surprise and she caught the giant off balance. His head shot forward and became wedged in the beehive. There was a pause, then a fierce buzzing from within the hive. Another moment's silence. Then Leif exploded in a torrent of pain.

"Oww! Yargh! Get them off me!" He danced around crazily, his huge hands clawing at his hair and sticky beard.

Eoin and Derval knew they were in great danger but they couldn't help giggling at how helpless and silly the giant looked. Some of his own men also had great difficulty in stifling giggles.

"Toren! Toren! Where are you, stupid ox? I can't see a thing and these bees are killing me!" Leif whined as he stumbled around blindly.

"Here, Leif!" Toren took his arm and guided him forward. "The stream, Leif. Into the stream! It's your only hope!" Leif needed no encouragement. There was a mighty splash as he fell face forward into the stream and struggled to keep his head under water. The children's giggles had grown to open laughter now but the laughter died when Toren grabbed each of them roughly by the arm.

□

Leif emerged from the stream, spluttering, shivering and shaking his head violently. "W-where are th-those b-brats?" he croaked.

"Here Leif," Toren announced, "I have them!"

"W-well t-tie them up so they c-can't play any m-more of their tricks on me. Bah! N-nobody has g-given me so much t-trouble since I c-came to this c-country!"

Toren wasted no time carrying out his master's orders. It was not a time to upset him further.

"Ouch!" Derval squealed. "That rope hurts!" She aimed a kick at Toren's shin but he skipped out of her way.

"What are the rest of you staring at?" Leif barked. "Get a fire going. Burn anything that burns. I'm f-freezing!"

The children were now firmly bound and were tied to each other. "Eoin, what are we going to do?" Derval whispered. "We promised Brother Killian we would keep the gold cross safe and now that one-eyed monster has it!"

"There isn't much we can do, tied up like this," Eoin replied.

"Well maybe when they leave, we could follow them..."

"To Dyfflin?"

"Yes—and somehow get the cross back before he melts it!"

"But Dyfflin is a long way—and we don't even know what it's like, except that it's full of Norsemen like Leif."

"Bad luck to them!" Derval growled. "But we must do something."

"Well maybe we'll be going to Dyfflin anyway," her brother mused.

"What do you mean?"

"I mean as slaves."

"As slaves?" Derval shouted, forgetting her situation.

"Shush, Derval. Don't give them ideas!"

"But I'm only twelve and you're only ten!" Derval whispered, aghast.

"That won't stop them! I've heard they sell slaves of all ages."

"Well maybe if we annoy Leif enough he'll be glad to leave us behind. I have another little trick in mind for him when…"

Their conversation was interrupted by Toren, who bundled them back towards the church. A large fire was already blazing. Leif pranced up and down in front of it. "Throw some more wood on that fire!" he roared. "I must dry out before we leave this place. My face is on fire with bee-stings!" His warriors could see that Leif's face was already a mass of red weals. Somebody giggled. Leif spun around. "What are you lot laughing at? I'll run my sword through the next man I see even smiling! Get to work, you lazy clods!"

The warriors turned away as if they themselves had been stung. "Toren? Toren!" Leif bellowed. "Why is that oaf never here when I need him?"

"Here I am, Leif!" Toren bounded forward. "Just making sure those children don't cause you any more trouble!"

"Brats!" Leif spat the word out but did not look at the two prisoners. He turned again to Toren. "What spoils do we have? You'd better have some good news for me!"

"Well we have some small bits of silver—not much I'm afraid! The monks must have taken most of the valuables with them to the tower."

"Bah! I told those fools to prevent the monks getting to the tower! What else?"

"There are books, beautifully written and illustrated. Look!" Toren handed some loose pages of vellum to Leif.

"Books! Books!" He glared at the unfortunate Toren. "What use are books to me?" He paused to look at the vellum sheets and then tossed them on to the fire. "At least they'll burn well," he laughed.

"No! No!" Derval screamed. "You can't do that! They are sacred books. The monks spent years copying them."

"Quiet, brat!" Leif hissed, "or you'll be next for the fire! What else, Toren?"

"Well, there are the pigs."

"Round them all up and put them into a cart but kill one first. We must eat before we leave this miserable place. It was hardly worth the journey from Dyfflin for this lot."

"I already have a pig roasting for you," said Toren, who knew his master well, "and you forget the gold cross," he continued, hoping that Leif would not also forget the reward.

"I suppose you are right, Toren. Let me have another look at it." He reached inside his tunic and drew out the gold cross. He twirled it about in his hand. "Yes! Yes! I can see my beautiful Helga will like this almost as much as she likes me. She will be pleased!"

"Hah!" Eoin scoffed. "How could anyone like a wild boar like him!"

Derval agreed. "Imagine having to kiss a face like that!"

Leif was too busy examining the cross to hear them. "Yes, I'll bring this to Magnus the goldsmith when we return to Dyfflin. He'll melt it down and make a fine brooch for Helga."

"That's sinful," Eoin protested. "You can't do that to a sacred cross. God will punish you for that!"

"Can't I?" Leif thundered. "Nobody says Leif can't do

something and nobody punishes Leif! Nobody. Except those bees," he muttered.

"And St Killian," Derval added.

"St Killian? What's that?" Leif asked.

"St Killian was the holy man who founded this monastery," Derval stole a wink at Eoin. "And it's said he will put a curse on anyone who attacks his monastery."

"Bah. Nonsense!" Leif laughed.

"We'll see," said Derval calmly. "If we call on him, he'll punish you!"

"Hah! Let him just try!"

Derval looked up at the round tower.

"Killian!" she called. "Killian, are you listening?" She paused and then added to Leif's puzzlement by speaking in Latin, a language he could not understand but which Eoin and Derval had picked up from the monks. Eoin smiled at his sister's latest trick. She really is far too clever for Leif, he thought, and then added his voice to Derval's chant.

Leif swaggered about at the base of the tower, shaking his head. "Foolish brats!" he laughed. "What a strange country this is. And such a strange language those children are speaking!" He turned to Toren. "Where's that pig you were to roast for me? I'm hungry and we must get out of this crazy place soon!"

Toren went in search of the roast pig. Leif noticed that the children had stopped chanting. He turned to them. "Well? What happened to your Killian?" he mocked. "Did he not listen to you?"

"Oh yes he did," Derval said confidently. "Look up at the tower!"

Leif looked up, open-mouthed. The door slid back silently and before Leif realised what was happening, a torrent of scalding water descended on him. "Oooh! Ahhh!" he yowled, dancing about, as he shook his head and arms as if to wriggle free from the intense pain. He pranced around for a few minutes, screaming abuse at everyone who stood watching him. Above him the door closed silently.

Derval smiled. "Thank you, Killian," she called.

"My face! My hands!" Leif moaned. "First the bees and now this!" He marched over to the children, reaching for his sword. Derval and Eoin huddled together, trembling. "I hate you two!" Leif shouted, holding the massive sword above them. "I have a mind to carve you into pieces and leave you for the wolves!"

The children cowered beneath him, fearing the worst. There was a moment's pause. It seemed an eternity to the children. "But no!" Leif said at last, dropping his voice suddenly. "Instead I will have my revenge! I'm taking you with me to Dyfflin! I can get good money by selling you as slaves. Hah! How do you feel about that, brats?"

Just then two of his warriors appeared, carrying a roast pig on a long pole. "Bah! There's no time for that now," Leif snapped, but not before he had sliced a leg off the pig for himself. He pushed one of the warriors roughly aside, causing the pig to fall into the nearby fire. "Come! We must leave this miserable place at once!" he mumbled, as he stuffed his mouth with pig-meat. "Toren! Put those two in with the pigs and see how they like that!"

The children were quickly bundled into the cart alongside the screaming frightened pigs and within minutes the Viking procession—horses, carts and warriors on foot—was making its way out of the settlement and back towards Dyfflin. The noise in the cart was deafening. Every few minutes the cart-wheels would hit a rock or sink in a hollow and children and pigs were jolted all around the cart. Eoin and Derval were still tied together and could not protect themselves from the trampling pigs.

"I'm frightened, Derval," Eoin sobbed.

"So am I," his sister shouted back. "But if we stay together we'll be all right!"

"We can't do much else, tied up like this. I hope we don't end up like these poor pigs!"

"Don't even say that, Eoin!"

"But what will happen to us in Dyfflin, Derval? Will that one-eyed monster really sell us as slaves?"

Derval strained to sit upright and look back at the monastery. The cart was trundling down a steep hill and slowly the round tower disappeared from view. "I don't know," she said quietly. "I don't know."

4

A Viking Procession

The cart reached even ground and, except for an odd snort, the pigs settled down and lay still. Derval and Eoin sat upright, back to back. Neither spoke for some time. There was nothing to say. They could only wonder about their fate. Derval looked at the pigs. "I envy you," she thought. "At least you don't worry about what's going to happen to you. And when it does happen, it's over quickly." She shuddered. Eoin thought of their home, of their mother watching out for them, their father noticing the smoke coming from the monastery and wondering…

The light was beginning to fade. The countryside was no longer familiar to them. The procession followed a rough track which had been cleared through woods. Eoin broke the silence.

"Derval?"

"Yes."

"If we're sold as slaves we could be sold separately, couldn't we?"

"Suppose so."

"That means we might never see each other again."

"Mmm."

"Don't you care?"

"Of course I care, silly. But right now I'm watching a very hungry pig eat through the rope in the corner."

"If only he would eat our ropes we could try to make a run for it."

"Maybe we could still try."

"How?"

"If we could force the cart open where the pig has eaten through and let the pigs out..."

"They would cause such a panic that we might not be noticed."

"Exactly! It's worth a try! Come on, Eoin. Push me against the end of the cart!"

Eoin found it hard to get a proper grip. He slithered among the pigs until he could wedge his foot against a board in the floor of the cart. He then heaved against his sister, who jabbed at the tail-end of the cart with both feet. Her light sandals gave little protection to her feet, and with each jab she winced as a sharp pain shot through the soles of her feet. She was just about to give up when she felt the board give way and drop to the ground. She wasted no time in forcing a pig through the opening. Eoin swivelled around and sent another two pigs slithering through the gap. The rest of the pigs soon followed in a mad scramble to be free.

"Come on," Derval whispered. "Now it's our turn." They lay on their backs, wriggled feet-first through the gap and fell in a heap on the ground outside.

A voice cried out in the dusk. "Leif! Leif! The children! The pigs!" More shouts followed and the squeals of the freed pigs added to the confusion.

"Come on, Eoin. If we can get to the woods..." Derval panted. It was a hopeless task. Being tied together meant they couldn't both run in the same direction and whatever chance they had was ruined when they tripped over a pig.

"Stupid, stupid pig," Derval cried. "Away with you! At least you can run free."

A rough hand grabbed her ear and almost tore it off.

"Hah! Thought you would escape did you?" Leif raised his voice. "I have the brats! Stop those pigs! Catch them before they get to the woods! Hurry, you useless layabouts!"

The warriors did their best but the pigs had the scent of freedom and were not going to be stopped. They weaved and darted this way and that, escaping the flailing arms of the Norsemen before reaching the safety of the wood. Toren turned to Leif, breathless. "It's—it's no use, Leif. The pigs are too clever for us!"

Leif was furious. "Fools! Fools! You're right. The pigs are cleverer than you! Bah! I curse the day I met you two." He wrenched at an ear of both children. "My face and hands ache with bee-stings! Now I've lost the pigs for my wedding feast! I tell you this, you pair of troublemakers, Leif will have the last laugh. I still have the gold cross and I still have you two! I'll make sure to get an extra special price for you as slaves. Toren! Put them back in the cart and this time get in there yourself and watch them. If they cause any more trouble you lose your flask of wine. Understood?" Toren nodded. "And hurry! We must get to Dyfflin before dark! Hurry."

5

Dyfflin

The procession continued on its way in silence. Without the weight of the pigs, the cart bounced up and down on the rough track. Inside, the two prisoners were jolted hither and thither. "I'm sorry now we haven't got the pigs for company," Eoin complained. "It was more comfortable when they were in here with us."

"Well I'm not sorry," Derval answered, through gritted teeth. "I'm delighted we got the pigs away from that one-eyed monster! Just to show him he can't have his way in everything!" She peered into the growing dusk through the bars of the cart.

"Can you see anything out there?" Eoin asked.

"Very little. It's almost dark. There are no houses. But there's lots of smoke."

"We must be near Dyfflin. That's where the smoke is coming from. Can you not see any houses at all?"

Derval squinted to her right. "No. There's some sort of rampart blocking the view." She paused. "Listen!" A strange mixture of sounds drifted on the evening air. Men shouting, the barking of dogs, an occasional squeal from a pig, children laughing and calling, the clanging of barrels. "Dyfflin must be just beyond the rampart," Derval suggested.

"I don't like the sound of it," Eoin said quietly. "I'm frightened!"

"There's nothing to be frightened about," Derval replied sharply, trying to convince herself as much as her brother.

"Yes there is," Eoin countered. "Remember when Uncle Hugh drove his cattle to Dyfflin? He nearly got lost! He said there were hundreds of houses there. And all sorts of strangers who spoke in different tongues. And huge ships down at the river."

"Shush!" his sister jabbed her elbow into his back. The cart had come to a stop.

A voice rang out. "Halt! Who goes there?"

"Bah! Don't you recognise one of your own, idiot? It is I, Leif!" came the gruff reply.

"Sorry, friend. The light is fading and I have to be careful. Was your visit to the monastery a success?"

"Yes. I'm thinking of becoming a holy monk!" Leif growled.

"Hah! That would be a sight to see!" the guard laughed. "The mighty Leif in a monk's habit! Come on then— what have you got in the cart?"

"Don't remind me!" Leif barked. "It was full of nice fat pigs for my wedding feast until that pair of brats set them free. And that's all I got for my trouble—that pair and a few bits and pieces—one nice piece of gold for my beautiful Helga. That reminds me, I must be on my way to see Magnus the goldsmith."

"Better hurry then, Leif. The night draws in and Magnus will be leaving his work aside for a flask of wine. A ship came in today with several barrels."

"Hmph! He will work for me first!" The cart moved on a short distance and then came to a sudden halt. The back of the cart was quickly removed. "Come on, you two!" Leif snapped. "Out and walk! But first, in case you have any more ideas about escaping..." He dangled a heavy chain in front of the children and bent down to attach one end of it to Eoin's ankle, "this will make sure you don't wander very far!" He clamped the other end of the chain around Derval's ankle.

The guard watched Leif with growing curiosity. "Ho! What a fine pair of slaves you've got there, Leif! They must have put up a great struggle. I've never seen you come back with so many bruises and weals."

Leif brushed the guard aside. "It wasn't them," he mumbled. "It was bee...I-I mean I must be off. Goodnight!" He placed a hand on each of the children's shoulders and propelled them forward. "Hurry, you two! I must get to Magnus's house. Move!" As they stumbled forward, the children heard the mocking laughter of the guard recede in the darkness.

Although the darkness confused and frightened them and Leif bullied them into hurrying along despite their chains, Derval and Eoin were still able to take in something of their strange new surroundings. To their left they could just make out the silhouettes of several huge ships gently riding on the black waters of the river. They paused to gaze open-mouthed at such giant craft. They had never seen anything bigger than a curragh on the lake at Killadoo.

"This way!" Leif wheeled them away from the river and again shoved them forward. They were walking up a gentle slope now. The road beneath their feet was made of logs. It took some time for the children to accustom themselves to the logs and they stumbled frequently, particularly when a figure brushed past them in the gloom, or a dog snapped at their heels. On each side of them was a row of houses, with low log walls and thatched roofs. Occasionally, through an open door, the children could see figures moving about in the glow of a fire. Outside many of the houses, cattle or pigs were cramped in pens. All about them was noise.

"I've never heard so much noise in my life!" Eoin whispered.

"And so many houses. So many buildings in one place!" Derval added in amazement.

"I wish we were back in Killadoo just to hear the birds singing in the trees," Eoin sighed.

"You'd never hear a bird sing in this place, that's for sure." Derval gave a nervous laugh. She scrunched up her nose. "And as for that smell! Phew! Where is it coming from?"

A strange female voice interrupted them. "Well, if it isn't Leif of the One Eye! Have you no time to talk to your friends?"

"What? Oh hello, Solveig. I'm in a hurry!"

"Look Eoin," Derval whispered, "now I know where that smell is coming from!" She nodded towards a bucket which the woman was carrying. As if she had heard Derval, the woman grabbed the bottom of the bucket and cast its contents into a foul-smelling pit just inside a wattle fence that was beside the children. Derval leaped sideways as some of the contents splashed towards her. If it smelled that bad, she didn't want it near her.

"Ho! What a frightened pair of rabbits you have there, Leif!" the woman laughed. "Did you catch them on your trip to the countryside?"

"You might say that! Now I must hurry to Magnus's house."

"Oh you have work for Magnus?"

"I might."

"Mmm. Very secretive, aren't we? Well then, I won't tell you about my work for Helga."

"Oh, so it's you who are making her wedding dress!"

"I might," Solveig laughed mockingly as she moved away.

"Curious old chatterbox!" Leif grumbled. "Get a move on, you two!"

"I feel sick, Eoin," Derval whined. "Did you see the pit where she emptied the bucket?"

"Yes, and there's one outside every house! What a stinking place this Dyfflin is! Who would want to live here!"

"Come on!" Leif barked. "Move along and stop your chattering!"

They blundered their way along the ever-darkening but still noisy street. Curious faces peered across fences at them while children of their own age laughed and teased them before Leif cuffed their ears and sent them home whinging.

At last Leif steered them down a narrow pathway towards a dimly lit house. Before they reached the house, the sound of tuneless singing reached their ears. Leif swore and aimed a kick at the wattle fence. "I'm too late," he grunted. "The old fool has got the wine!" He hustled the children through the doorway. The dying embers of a fire glowed in the centre of the floor. It took some time for Derval and Eoin to adjust to the light. Poor though it was, it was a welcome change from the dark outside. Their eyes smarted as a mist of smoke drifted past them to the open door. On one side of the fire a low table was laden with an assortment of metal pieces, hammers of various sizes, tongs, knives and a sharpening stone. On a little tray lay a collection of buckles and brooches. On the other side a figure rested on a raised bed which was covered in straw.

"Ah Leif, my friend! Welcome! Come and join me!" The man swung his legs off the bed and rose unsteadily on his feet. A leather flask dangled from one hand.

"I will not join you, you drunken old fool. I have brought important work for you and now I see you are not fit to work!"

"What work, O one-eyed one? Your humble servant will attend to it...as soon as...well...in the morning, maybe.." He attempted to straighten up but his legs buckled under him and he grabbed at a post for support.

Leif was furious. "I'll come back in the morning then, when you're sober, you babbling old wine-flask!"

"Don't be so hard on poor old Magnus, Leif! Magnus works hard. Magnus is the best silversmith in Dyfflin! Look at my beautiful bracelets and fasteners! Look, children! Who are these children, Leif?" the puzzled Magnus asked.

"Just a couple of brats for the slave market," Leif replied impatiently. He was anxious to get away from the drunken old man.

"You'll get a quick sale for them down at the waterfront!" Magnus's eyes sparkled as he looked the children up and down. Eoin stepped back from him in fear. "There's a big ship just arrived from the warm lands of the south."

Leif looked at the leather flask now swinging wildly from Magnus's arm. "With a cargo of wine, obviously," he said with a sneer.

"That's true, and good wine it is too, I have to say, but that ship will be returning soon with slaves for the eastern lands! I spoke with its skipper."

Leif was suddenly very interested in the old man. "That's the first bit of sensible talk I've heard from you this night, old man. I'll go there in the morning and I'll be back to you with a very special piece of gold-work."

"Gold?" the old man rubbed his hands in glee. "I haven't worked with gold for an age."

"But only if you're sober," Leif cautioned. "Otherwise I go to Lars."

"Lars!" the old man thundered. "That fellow could not tie two pieces of straw together."

"But at least he remains sober."

"All right, all right!" the old man flapped his hands up and down. "I'll be ready for work—in the morning."

"Good! Come, you two. I'm tired and sore. It has been a difficult day. Tonight you stay with me. Tomorrow I'll be rid of you!" He shoved them out on to the street again. There was less noise now. An occasional bark. Voices raised in anger. They reached the top of the slope and found themselves on a wider street running across the top. Leif guided them to the left. "Not far now!" he mumbled. Derval and Eoin were by now limping from the heavy chain which chafed their ankles. Then they heard a low, vicious growl. They froze as a great dark hulk advanced towards them.

Leif stepped past the children. "Ah! I know I'm home when I hear Wolf's welcome!" The animal bared his huge teeth in a vicious snarl. "Quiet, boy. It's Leif!" The dog relaxed, trotted towards its master and stood on its hind legs, offering its forepaws in greeting. "Look! I've brought two prisoners for you to mind! Wolf likes minding prisoners, don't you boy?" The dog dropped back on all fours and began to snarl again. The children stepped back. "All right, Wolf!" Leif smiled. "I think they understand."

6

Helga

A tall slender figure emerged from Leif's house. "Leif! Leif! My great warrior has come home!"

"Helga! What a pleasant surprise! Ah my beautiful one! Come to me!" They kissed and embraced for a long time. Eoin poked at the ground with his toe in embarrassment.

"Leif!" Helga shrieked. "What has happened to your face? It's covered with sores!" She drew away from Leif, who turned from her in an effort to conceal his swollen face.

"It's...it's nothing! I...had some trouble with...with bees," he muttered.

"With bees?" Helga asked, shaking her head in mystification. "The mighty Leif had trouble with bees?" She exploded into laughter. "Bees...Leif?" she repeated over and over in disbelief. As Helga tossed her long flaxen hair over her shoulders, Derval caught a glimpse of her face in the firelight. Her fine sharp features stood out in silhouette. Her sparkling eyes danced with laughter.

What could a beautiful woman like her see in a brute like that, Derval wondered.

The "brute" suddenly changed mood and snarled at

Helga. "'Tis not a laughing matter, woman! Come. I'm hungry. Is there food?"

"Of course!" Helga's laughter subsided very quickly. "I should know better than to tease a hungry bear. I've got a fish stew bubbling on the fire—it's your favourite!" She looked over Leif's shoulder. "Are these your friends?" she asked, gesturing towards the children.

"Friends? No. Two troublemakers I'll be glad to be rid of in the slave market tomorrow. Come! Come! I am hungry." They all moved inside.

Leif's house was much bigger than Magnus's. In the centre, a bright fire hissed and spat and a cauldron bubbled and overflowed on to the burning wood below. On each side of the fire the floor was raised to a higher level by large sods of earth covered by straw and wood shavings. One of these areas was covered again by thick fleeces and it was here that Leif threw his sword and tunic before marching over to a dark corner to relieve himself. Helga busied herself in another corner before emerging with an armful of drinking vessels and a jug of milk. She smiled at the children and then noticed the chains. "Oh Leif, they are so young and you have them in chains!"

"I tell you, woman, they need to be in chains! Don't be deceived by their appearance!" He emerged from the shadows. "And must I say it again? I am hungry!" he bellowed.

"Oh all right, you big bear!" Helga dropped the vessels with a clatter. She picked up a large battered wooden bowl and ladled stew from the steaming cauldron into it until the bowl overflowed. "Here!"

She offered the bowl to Leif who grabbed it and began to slurp the stew greedily, pausing only to wipe the dribbles from his beard and mutter "Good! Good!"

Helga turned to the children. "Now, let me take those chains off. You look so frightened. What are your names?" The children whispered their names. They too were tired and hungry. "Der-val and Eo-in," Helga repeated to herself as she struggled to release the clamps on the children's ankles. "There!" she sighed as the clamps opened at last. The children immediately bent to rub some ease into their raw ankles. "You must be hungry too!" Helga said softly. "You shall have some of Helga's stew."

"No!" Leif mumbled and spluttered, holding out his near-empty bowl. "First you fill my bowl."

"Oh Leif," Helga said, filling his bowl from the cauldron, "you are such a beast!" She slammed the bowl down in front of him. "Maybe that will keep the bear from growling!"

"And wine! I must have wine! There's a flask hanging from the roof!" Helga flashed a vicious look at him but she did as he commanded. She turned to the children. "Now Der-val and Eo-in. Have I got the names right? Have some stew and something to drink." She handed each of them two small bowls—one of stew and one of milk. Eoin looked doubtfully at the stew and then at Derval, but hunger overcame them and they both gulped the stew.

"Ugh!" Derval spat most of the mouthful out again. "What is that?" she spluttered, taking a drink of milk to try to rid her mouth of the taste.

"It's mussel stew," the puzzled Helga answered, "my special mussel stew. Don't you like it?"

Eoin swallowed his mouthful with some difficulty. "We've never tasted anything like that before," he mumbled, "but we're hungry."

Helga laughed loudly. "You'll get used to it. Like my

big bear here!"

Leif belched and handed Helga an empty bowl. "More! More stew, woman!" He belched again.

Helga filled his bowl a third time. "You eat like a pig, Leif."

"Pigs! Don't talk to me about pigs!" he muttered between slurps. "I had a cart full of them for our wedding feast until—ah never mind, you would not understand!" He buried his face in the bowl again.

"So all you brought back is these two children and a face full of bee-stings," Helga laughed.

"No, silly woman, that's *not* all I brought back." Leif ran his huge fingers around the inside of the bowl and licked them clean. "I have a special gift for you on our wedding day but if you go on making fun of me there will be no gift—and no wedding!"

Helga pouted. "Oh, my big bear is angry. Helga is sorry. Here!" She smoothed out the fleeces on the bed. "Lie down and rest. You have had a bad day."

Leif stretched out his giant frame. "Maybe you're right. I feel sleepy."

"Anyway I must get back to my father's house," Helga said, turning to the children. "What about our two little friends?"

"We're not your friends," Derval snapped. "He took us prisoner—and he stole the go—"

"Quiet, brat!" Leif interjected, sitting upright again. "You go, Helga. They will stay here. Wolf will watch them." Helga turned to go and then paused. "What is it now, woman?" Leif asked impatiently.

Helga gently massaged Leif's shoulders. "It's that girl, Derval," she said softly. "I like her. She's got...spirit."

"Hmph!" Leif rubbed his aching face. "She certainly

has."

"And she reminds me of my young sister at home in the north lands. Could I have her as a servant? A wedding present," she added hastily.

"You're being foolish, woman. She will only cause trouble, I know!" He rubbed his face again.

"No, I can handle her. Can I have her please, my big bear?" Helga pleaded.

"Well, don't say I didn't warn you!"

Helga hugged and kissed Leif. "Oh thank you, Leif. You are so kind. You make Helga happy. You—"

"Just go, woman, and let me get my sleep. I will leave the girl at your house tomorrow on my way to the waterfront with the boy."

"I go, I go," Helga skipped out with the delight of a young child on her face. Leif lay back and closed his one eye.

"Where do we sleep?" Derval yawned.

"What is wrong with the floor? You're lucky to have a roof over your heads." Leif did not even open his eye. "And don't even think of escaping!" he added in the same sleepy voice. "If you put your nose outside the door, Wolf will bite it off! Now I go to sleep."

Too upset and frightened even to whisper, the children curled up on the other side of the fire from Leif and tried to make themselves as comfortable as possible. It wasn't easy as the layer of wood shavings on the floor only barely covered several large and uneven paving stones. Derval cupped her hands beneath her head and reflected on the events of the day. It seemed an age since she and Eoin had raced each other to the monastery at Killadoo. She wondered if the brothers were safe and how they were coping with the destruction the Norsemen had left behind. She wondered about her own parents, who would be anxiously searching for their children. Tears welled up in her eyes. She glanced sideways at her brother, fearful he might see her crying. She smiled. Eoin's heavy breathing told her that he was already asleep. She envied him. Exhaustion had overcome his discomfort.

She squirmed this way and that in an effort to get comfortable. It was impossible. To add to her troubles, she found she was scratching herself furiously. The fleas weren't sleeping either! She lay on her back again. That smell! It drifted all about her. "The pigs have cleaner houses in Killadoo," Derval thought. Killadoo. Would they ever see it again? She rolled over to the wall of the house and forced the wattles apart. A vicious snarl warned her to push them together again. That dog must never sleep either! To complete her misery, Leif began to snore. It was like a thunderstorm each time the sleeping giant drew a long breath through his nose and then expelled it through his quivering lips. Derval jammed her palms against her ears but it was useless. The whole house seemed to shake each time Leif snored.

Derval sat upright and looked at the great shadowy bulk that lay on the bed opposite. "Big bear is right," she thought. "If only I could get the gold cross back from him at least..." She had noticed him put the precious bundle under his head before he settled down to sleep. She could not possibly move him from his present position. "But there must be a way," she thought, "there must." She thought of Brother Killian and old Brother Cormac. Moving stealthily so as not to disturb the dozing Wolf, she picked up a wood shaving, edged closer to Leif and began to tickle his nose...

7

The Cornmarket

Shafts of morning sunlight playing through the wattles of the wall woke Derval. Sleep had come to her eventually but it seemed only an hour since she had nodded off. She opened one eye. Eoin was still asleep beside her. She turned her head slowly towards the other side of the house. Leif was moving about, mumbling to himself. Derval watched as he felt inside his tunic, looked puzzled for a moment, then searched where his head had lain the previous night and smiled as he picked up a small bundle wrapped in cloth. Derval held her breath for a moment when it seemed as if Leif was about to unwrap the bundle. He hesitated and stuffed it inside his tunic instead. Derval smiled and closed her eyes.

A few moments later, Leif shook her roughly. "Come on, you two. It's time to go. The best prices in the slave market are to be had early in the day." Eoin yawned and stretched himself. "I see you slept well in Leif's house."

"Leif's pigsty," Derval muttered.

Leif picked up a breadcake, broke it in two, broke one half in two again and tossed a portion to each of the children while he crammed the rest into his mouth. "Some rye bread!" he mumbled. "It's all the food there is."

Derval bit into the bread. It was as hard as the stone she sat on. Her stomach ached with hunger but she could not even break the bread into crumbs.

"Come! We must hurry!" Leif stood above them. They rose slowly, bones stiff from lying on the hard ground. Leif pushed them through the doorway, where Wolf lay, giving low growls. "Stay, Wolf!" Leif commanded. "Stay and guard Leif's house." The children walked nervously around the dog. Eoin dropped his rye bread beside Wolf. In a moment he had swept it into his powerful jaws. One chomp, one gulp and the bread was gone.

"If you want to use the cesspit, do so, but hurry!" Leif snapped. Derval and Eoin looked at each other. They could not even bear to approach the pit. "Well come on then!" Leif said. "First to Helga's house. It's just past the Cornmarket."

Dyfflin in the daylight was an amazing sight to the children: the people, the bustle, the cries, the noise caused them to turn in every direction in open-mouthed amazement. Children ran about the street in play, sometimes pausing to stare with curiosity at the strangers and to tease and poke fun at them. Smoke billowed through the roofs of houses as the day's work began. In front of one house, a smith stood by a roaring fire, turning an iron bar in the flames, then pulling it out and hammering and shaping the glowing end of the bar. The children had to jump aside as a herd of frightened, squealing pigs swept past them. The town was alive with people and industry. A carpenter hammered and sawed; merchants shouted their wares to passing traders; in a compound, weavers and spinners worked ceaselessly. People exchanged greetings. So many people. So much noise. Derval constantly tripped over the street-logs as she tried to take in the clamour and confusion that was all around. And all the time Leif hustled and harried them.

They came to a long low building at the bottom of the street. A few carts were lined up outside, loaded with sacks of grain and flour. "The Cornmarket," Derval thought. It was a large covered area with no walls, just pillars to support the roof. Inside, she could see sacks being exchanged, deals being done. Outside, the farmers waited patiently by their carts. Suddenly Eoin tugged at Derval's sleeve. "Look!" he whispered excitedly. "That man with the second cart! I know him. We met him—"

"At the monastery!"

Derval nodded, her heart beating wildly. She and Eoin looked at each other, then together they shouted at the man. "Hey! Killadoo! Killadoo!" The man and his helper looked around in puzzlement. Encouraged, the children shouted even louder. "Diarmuid's children! Killadoo! Prisoners!" The two men, taken by surprise, strained to hear and to see who was shouting at them.

"What are you two brats shouting about?" Leif thundered, his face red with rage and embarrassment. "Stop that shouting!" He cuffed each of them on the back of the head. "Move! Helga's house is just down here!" he shoved them onwards.

Derval glowered back at Leif, rubbing her head. "Big, ugly pig!" she muttered under her breath. Leif shook his fist at her.

"Do you think they recognised us?" Eoin whispered.

"I don't know. I don't know! I just hope so," Derval replied, looking back anxiously towards the Cornmarket.

Leif shepherded the children down a pathway towards a large house just beyond the Cornmarket. The plot in front of the house was littered with barrels, buckets and churns at different stages of manufacture. In the middle of the plot a tall lean man struggled to tighten a hoop on a large barrel. He paused to wipe his brow and noticed the visitors approaching.

"Greetings Leif! I see you bring help for poor Erik!" he joked.

"They're for the slave market!" Leif barked. "Is Helga inside?"

"She is, she is—unfortunately. The sooner you take her off my hands, the better! What with the excitement of the wedding, never mind the cost, it's all too much for a poor cooper. I think I'll take up slave-trading like you, Leif!"

"I wouldn't advise it," Leif snapped and then muttered, "Poor cooper! There's no such thing as a poor cooper in Dyfflin. Old tightwad!" For a moment Derval forgot her situation and smiled. "Helga!" Leif roared as he entered the house. "Come, woman, I'm in a hurry."

Helga bounded towards Leif and threw her arms about him. "You are always in a hurry, my big bear! And how are the bee-stings today?"

Leif pushed her away. "Do not tease Leif, woman," he snapped, glowering at her.

Helga sulked for a moment before she noticed the children. She brightened up at once. "Ah, here is Derval! See, I remembered your name!" She held her arms out in greeting but Derval did not move. The moment she had been dreading had arrived. "Come, Derval. You must meet my family," Helga said very softly. "Come, there is nothing to fear!"

"I-I'm not afraid," Derval stammered. "I must say goodbye to my b-brother."

Helga nodded. "All right, I understand."

Derval turned to Eoin. The tears welled up in her eyes and in her brother's too. Derval fought back the sobs that almost choked her voice. "It will be all right, Eoin. Helga will...treat me...well...and...we'll...meet...again...soon."

Eoin dropped his head and stared at the ground. "Will we?" he asked despondently. Derval knew what he was thinking. Soon he would be sent to a far-off country and they would almost certainly never see each other again.

"Of course we will!" she comforted him, although she did not believe it herself. She put her arms around her brother and held him very tightly. She felt his warm tears on her shoulder. "Race you back...to...Killadoo!" she whispered. The mention of their native place caused her to swallow hard. Eoin pressed his head against her shoulder.

"Oh come on, you two. Stop snivelling!" Leif growled impatiently. "Come, boy!" He grabbed Eoin's wrist roughly. "We must get to the waterfront!" He half-dragged him out onto the street.

Eoin looked back in desperation at his sister. "Goodbye Derval," he cried.

"Goodbye Eoin—and God protect you!"

8

The Hammer of Thor

Soon Helga and Derval were out of sight. Leif's grip on
Eoin's wrist did not ease for the remainder of the journey.
Within minutes they reached the huge earthen bank
which separated the town from the river. They walked a
short distance along the foot of the bank until they came
to a large gateway. Leif marched through the gateway and
up a steep incline until at last they faced the river estuary.
Leif paused to get his bearings and Eoin stood bewildered
by the scene before him. He had never before seen such
a broad expanse of water. Even more astounding was the
sight of huge ships beached in a row along the mudflats
at the edge of the water, their great carved bows rising
into the sky like living creatures. He counted the ships
with nods of his head. One-two-three-four-five-six. Further
out on the water smaller fishing craft bobbed about in the
shadow of the giant ships. Along the shore various crafts-
men were busy at work. Shipbuilders and carpenters
hammered and sawed as they carried out repairs to
damaged craft. Nearby a cooper and his helper pulled a
cart on which three barrels rolled about. Leif approached
them.

"Here, cooper, I'm looking for a ship by the name of

The Hammer of Thor."

"Indeed I know it well! It came in only yesterday and the captain bought six of my fine barrels. I have some more barrels if you're looking—"

"No, fool! I'm looking for a ship!"

"All right! All right! A man has to earn his living. Let me see. It's the one-two-three-fourth ship down. We're on our way there with these barrels if you—"

Leif waited no longer but marched swiftly down the mudflat. Eoin had to trot along to keep up with his giant steps. They reached *The Hammer of Thor*. A man was inspecting the bow of the ship. Leif addressed him. "You would be the captain of this vessel?"

"I am that. Ragnar of the Seven Seas, they call me! And you?"

"Leif."

"And this is your boy?"

"No! No! He's just a br...He's a slave for sale—a fine strong young boy who will fetch a good price for you in some far-off land. You deal in slaves, I am told?"

The captain looked doubtful. "You are misinformed. I don't deal that much in slaves. Too much trouble. Wines, spices, fine silks, they're my business."

"Surely you could use him as a deck-boy on your ship and, if that didn't work out, you could sell him at the other end of your voyage."

"I don't know. He looks a bit sullen to me. Probably lazy too."

"Not at all! He's a great worker. Clever, too." Leif tightened his grip even more on Eoin's wrist. "I'll be sorry to lose him but a man's got to earn a living!" Eoin kicked him on the shin. The blow probably hurt Eoin more than it did Leif but Ragnar was quick to notice it. A severe frown darkened his face. "S-spirited too!" Leif hissed, almost wrenching Eoin's arm from its socket. "I like a lad with spirit, don't you?"

"I don't know," Ragnar stroked his beard. "I am a bit short-handed but he's very young. Maybe he's worth a try. What are you asking? If it's wine, I have none."

At this stage Leif would have gladly given Eoin away for nothing just to be rid of him but Ragnar saved him that embarrassment. "Some silks maybe? I have some fine silks over here." He gestured to Leif to follow him to a temporary shelter which he had constructed on the mudflat. As the two men inspected the rolls of silk, Leif absent-mindedly released his grip on Eoin. I could make a run for it now, Eoin thought. He looked around but could barely see over the earthen bank. But which way? There are so many streets. And what of Derval? I couldn't leave without her. Maybe if I hid.

Leif interrupted his thoughts by gripping Eoin's shoulder. "A deal then!" He sounded very pleased. "It is good doing business with you, Ragnar." He carried two rolls of silk under his arm.

"Hmph!" Eoin thought. "Is that all I'm worth?"

"I hope I won't regret it!" Ragnar said. "All right, boy—what's your name anyway?"

"Eoin."

"Eo-in. Strange name. Strange people! Your work will be to feed my men and keep my ship clean. You can start now with the cleaning. We sail tomorrow on the tide. Up you go, there!" He gestured to a rope ladder that hung over the bow. Leif gave Eoin an almost friendly cuff on the shoulder. "Good luck, lad," he said cheerily and then, bending down, he added with a hiss, "and good riddance!" Eoin climbed the ladder and as he descended into the ship his last view was of Leif striding down the mudflat with two rolls of silk under one arm and singing at the top of his voice.

Eoin's heart sank. He had finally been parted from his sister. Tomorrow he would sail in a Norse ship to a far-off land, perhaps to be sold and never to return to Killadoo. His only chance, remembering Leif's words, was to work hard as a deck-boy. In this way Ragnar would keep him rather than sell him. Some day, he hoped, Ragnar would return to Dyfflin, and then...

"To work, boy!" Ragnar thrust a broom into Eoin's hand. It was obvious that it had been a long time since anyone had taken a broom to these decks. They were littered with bones, stinking fish and other rotten food. Worst of all was a huge cauldron in the stern of the ship. The smell told Eoin that this cauldron was used as a cesspit. His stomach churned. "Clear up that mess before the crew returns," Ragnar ordered, "and empty the mess into that pot." Eoin sighed and began to work, sweeping between the benches towards the central passageway. It proved a futile exercise. Water lapped around his ankles when he stood in the passageway and each time he swept the debris towards it the whole mess slopped back between the benches again. Eoin was near to tears but he knew Ragnar was watching. There was nothing for it but to rake up the floating debris with his hands and dump it in the big pot. Progress was slow and as he worked his way towards the stern, the stench from the pot almost overpowered him. He cleaned up the deck as best he could and flopped down exhausted on a bench near the bow.

His eyes were about to close when a noisy clamour woke him. The crew of *The Hammer of Thor* was returning. They clambered noisily over the side. Some carried provisions for the journey: water, bread, salted meat. Others had difficulty in climbing the rope ladder. They must have drunk most of the wine they brought, Eoin thought. They were big, brawny men, all twenty of them, their tanned and weather-lined faces showing evidence of many years of sailing. Some of them, especially the drunken ones, pointed at Eoin and sniggered. Ragnar was none too pleased with the drunkards. He barked an order at four of them, who lumbered towards the cesspot and began to raise it towards the side of the ship. The intention was to empty its contents over the side but at a crucial stage one of the men began laughing. All four became giddy and in a moment, the pot was upended on top of them. There was uproar as the rest of the crew fell about in raucous laughter at the plight of their comrades.

Eoin didn't know whether to laugh or cry. It was a comical sight to watch but he also feared he would have to start the cleaning all over again. Ragnar was furious. He produced a leather whip and began to lash the unfortunate men, screaming at them all the while. To Eoin's relief the men began to clean up the mess, to the jibes of their comrades. Eventually at the second attempt, they tipped the contents of the pot over the side and at Ragnar's insistence they jumped into the water themselves to wash and rid themselves of the awful smell.

The afternoon dragged by as the crew prepared the ship for sailing. Eoin handed out a meal of bread and meat to the men, who ate with relish. Ragnar spoke sternly to them while they ate. It was clear that nobody was to leave the ship. As night approached most of the men stretched out on their benches and covered themselves with fleeces. A small group played a dice-game and argued constantly. Eoin huddled in the bow of the ship where the men had stored the food. He shivered in the cold night air until a huge heavy fleece descended on him. One of the dice-players smiled and winked at him. Eoin nodded his thanks. Warmth soon brought sleep.

He awoke to the easy sway of the ship and the sharp commands of Ragnar. He rubbed his bleary eyes and peered about him. It was barely light but the ship was full of activity. The crew members were poised on great oars, watching Ragnar. Eoin clambered on top of the stores and looked over the side of the ship. The mudflat had disappeared. The tide had come in and was lapping noisily against the earthen bank. Suddenly Ragnar barked an order and the men began to row, at first in an easy rhythm, then at an increased pace. *The Hammer of Thor* slid off her resting place and into deep water. Eoin had to hold on to the prow in order to keep his balance. At Ragnar's call, the men struck a steady rowing rate until they reached the middle of the channel. Then one half of the crew stopped rowing and the great ship slewed around, parallel with the shore. At a signal from Ragnar four men leaped to the mast and in seconds a huge white sail unfurled. The sail was secured and a light wind slowly filled it. The ship began to move down the river towards the open sea.

As it did so, reality caused terrible pangs to tear through Eoin's mind. Now at last it came home to him. No more Dyfflin. Killadoo no more. Derval never. His mother and father never. Never. Never again. He looked around desperately. The men rested as the full sail bore the ship towards the sea. "No," he whispered again and again. "No—!" he screamed and with arms and legs thrashing wildly, he jumped.

9

Olaf

The shock of hitting the water at speed seemed to suck the breath out of Eoin. The water stung the front of his body as he flopped awkwardly into it. Then he was beneath the surface flailing, fighting for his breath. He shot upwards and as his head broke the surface he gulped air. For a brief moment he was aware of men shouting before the current dragged him under again. He felt himself being propelled forward at a frightening speed. Eoin had only ever swum in the calm lake near Killadoo and this was terrifyingly different. He kicked and fought his way to the surface again, spat water and breathed in rapidly. A ringing went through his ears. Through a film of water he could see *The Hammer of Thor* quite some distance downriver. He felt terribly cold. He floundered and kicked until he could feel no sensation in his arms. He was going under again. Cold. He felt so cold. Down. Floating down. Fight! Could not fight any longer. Mud. Touching mud. See. Can't see.

He made a huge effort and once more his head rose above the surface. Light. Air. Must breathe. Must breathe. For an instant he caught a glimpse of something that moved on the river bank, it seemed like miles away. He managed a feeble wave.

On the river bank was a tall, gangling youth. "Thor and Odin! It's someone in the water!" He threw the rope of the net he was using in Eoin's direction. "Hang on to the rope!" he screamed. "I'll haul you in! The rope. The rope!"

Eoin was barely conscious of someone shouting. Rope. Can't see rope. He somehow found the strength to lift an arm. He felt the rough cords of a rope and weakly closed his fist about it. "Good," the youth cried. "Now just hang on and you'll be all right." The youth strained and hauled with all his strength. Once he had pulled Eoin clear of the current, it was easy enough to draw him through the shallows. He knelt, leaning over Eoin. "Are you all right?" he whispered nervously.

For a few frightening moments there was no reply. Then, "C-c-cold! So c-cold!"

"Here. Let me wrap my cloak about you. There. Now rest a while and then you can come to my house. It's only over there." He gestured towards the nearest street. He sat back on the mudflat, shook his head and laughed. "Phew! You're the biggest fish I've ever caught on a rope!" He watched as colour, warmth and a little strength slowly ebbed back into Eoin. "I'm Olaf," he said. "And you?"

"Eoin."

"So you are not Norse! How did you come to be in the river?"

"I...fell in!"

"Well you need to change those clothes and have a warm drink. Are you able to walk or will I carry you?"

"N-no!" Eoin shrank away from Olaf. "I'll go now. I'm all right. Thank you for rescuing me."

Olaf laughed loudly. "Where will you go? Look, I can see you are frightened, but there's nothing to be afraid of!

We won't harm you. There's only my mother and my brother and sister."

"But you're Norse!"

"So? We won't eat you!" Olaf laughed. "Come on. It's not far."

Eoin was still not convinced. "Do you know Leif of the one eye?"

"So that's why you are afraid! We know Leif all right, but don't worry. We hate him as much as you do!"

"Why would you hate him?"

"Because he killed my uncle, that's why! Now come, lean on my arm!" They struggled across the mudflat into the third house on the nearest street.

The first thing that Eoin noticed on entering the house was the smell. It was the pleasant smell of bread baking on the hearth, a smell that reminded him of home. After the glare of sunshine outside, he found it difficult to accustom his eyes to the dark and the smoke. He could see the figure of a woman bent over the fire. "Olaf? You're home early. Was the fishing so good?" She turned to greet her son. "My god, what have you got here, child!" she exclaimed on seeing the weak and bedraggled boy hanging on to her son's arm.

"This is Eoin. I fished him out of the river," Olaf said boastfully. "Eoin, this is my mother, Bríd."

"This is no time for introductions, boy," said Bríd, brushing her son aside. "Throw some wood on the fire!" She placed her hands on Eoin's shoulders and looked into his eyes. She had a kindly round face and spoke softly and with obvious concern for the boy. "God help you, child! You're perished with the cold and wet. Get these soaking clothes off you at once!"

"B-but!" Eoin stammered.

"No buts, boy. Get over to the fire and warm yourself!" She called to her son. "Olaf, find some dry clothes for this boy." Eoin squatted in front of the crackling fire and welcomed the heat that seeped into his bones. The woman busied herself in a corner of the house.

Eoin turned to her. "But you are Irish. Your name is Bríd!"

"Indeed, and what's strange about that?" She placed a small cooking pot beside the fire.

"You're here in Dyfflin with all these Norsemen."

Bríd laughed heartily. "Well with one of them, anyway! I am married to Bjorn, a fine man who is somewhere on the seas just now. He's on his way home with a cargo of pottery."

"But I thought..."

"You thought all Norsemen were wild savages," Bríd chortled.

"Like Leif!" Olaf added, handing a tunic and trousers to Eoin. "He had some trouble with the one-eyed one!"

"Oh! That rascal! He's a bad one, all right. We must hear your story, Eoin, but first some food. Sorcha, bring the cake!"

Eoin was startled to see another figure emerge from the shadows, a young girl, about his own age. She smiled shyly, handing a large cake to her mother.

"That's Sorcha, my only daughter," Bríd explained. "Bjorn and I agreed that the boys would have Norse names and the girls Irish names. So we have Sorcha and Olaf and Sven!"

"Sven?"

"That's our eldest boy. He will be here soon. Sorcha, will you not welcome Eoin to our house?" Sorcha blushed and greeted Eoin. He returned the greeting, still slightly confused. Bríd handed him a bowl of steaming hot milk and a large slice of the freshly baked cake.

Eoin relished the food. The milk was warming and the cake was delicious, hot and fresh and sweet. He savoured every crumb of it. Bríd read his mind. "I think our visitor likes our cake, Sorcha," she laughed and cut him an even bigger slice.

Eoin smiled in embarrassment. "Thank you," he mumbled through a mouthful of cake. "It's lovely!"

"It's good to see you smile, Eoin," Bríd said. "Now maybe you can tell us your story..."

10

Daithí Dall

Helga strode briskly down the street which led to the house of Solveig, the dressmaker. To her annoyance she had to check her stride every so often to beckon to Derval. "Come along, Derval. Why do you keep looking back?"

"I'm just wondering what ship Eoin is on or if he has gone already."

"He'll be all right. He's young and strong and clever. He will come back some day."

"But when?"

"Who knows? Come. Here we are." Helga stopped to enter a small house that was wedged in a narrow plot between two larger houses. "Greetings, Solveig," Helga called.

A short dumpy woman with a cheery smile emerged to meet them. "Ah Helga. You've come to see your wedding dress. And who is your little friend? Haven't I seen her before?"

"This is Derval. She works for me. Leif brought—"

"Of course. She was with Leif last night. What is wrong with that man, Helga? He is so impatient. Hasn't time to talk to anyone. Last night he was rushing to Magnus's house. Today he went rushing by me again. I tell you,

Helga, you will have a job taming that lion. He's always in a rage."

Helga laughed loudly. "Don't worry, I can manage him. Now, about the dress, Solveig?"

"Yes, yes, of course." She reached to take down a garment which had been hanging on the roof-pole. "It's not quite finished yet. Just a few little—"

"Oooh!" Helga sighed. "It's beautiful, Solveig. What do you think, Derval?" she turned excitedly to the girl who stood in the doorway.

"It's...nice," Derval muttered with a total lack of interest.

"Can I take it outside to see the colour in daylight?" Helga asked, brushing past Derval. She held the long royal blue woollen dress aloft by its shoulder straps. "It really is beautiful, Solveig. I can't wait."

Helga and Solveig were so occupied with the dress that they did not see Leif arriving. Suddenly he barged past his bride-to-be. "Out of my way!" he growled. "Where is she? The miserable little wretch! I'll...I'll feed her to my dog!"

Derval, who *had* noticed Leif's approach, stood trembling behind Helga, who was clearly annoyed at Leif's intrusion. "Leif, what on earth is the matter with you?" Helga snapped.

"Don't you know it is bad luck for the groom to see the bride's dress before the wedding?" Solveig asked.

Leif bristled with rage. "Bad luck? Bad luck? Don't talk to me about bad luck! I've had nothing but misfortune since I met those two brats in the monastery." He spied Derval cowering behind Helga. "Come on, you little wretch. Out with it, hand it over!" He held his great fist threateningly in mid-air. Derval backed away from him.

"Hand over what, Leif?" the puzzled Helga asked,

restraining him.

"She knows what I'm talking about!" Leif fumed, pointing at Derval, who took another few steps back until she realised she was at the edge of a cesspit.

"The shame of it!" Leif continued. "I go up to Magnus's house to explain what I want done. I unwrap the cloth and what do I find? This!" He reached into his tunic and produced a well-chewed bone. Helga began to titter behind her hand. "I can still hear Magnus laughing at me," Leif continued. "So hand it over, brat, before I hold you upside-down by the ankles and shake it out of you!"

"Leif!" Helga remonstrated.

"All right! All right!" Derval pleaded as the giant advanced towards her. "I have it here," she said reaching into a fold of her dress and trying desperately to think of a ruse to outwit Leif. She quickly withdrew something from her dress and held it behind her back. Suddenly she felt quite brazen. She looked up at Leif and calmly said, "I would rather let the cesspit have it than let you destroy it. So there!" She released the object from her hands. It plopped gently into the cesspit and quickly sank.

For a moment Leif was silent, mesmerised. He then turned to the two women and began to babble hysterically. "Did you see...look what she...you cursed little...did you...she...she threw it...in the cesspit!"

Helga could not help laughing. "Oh Leif, you should see the look on your face. It's so funny! Whatever it is you two are fighting over, it must be—"

"*Whatever* it is!" Leif spluttered. "Do you know what it is, you foolish woman? It is a gold cross which was going to be turned into your wedding gift! That's what it is!" He sank to his knees at the edge of the cesspit and peered in. "And now," he sobbed, "it's sinking into a cesspit!" He plunged his arm into the pit and furiously combed the stinking mess. "A cesspit—deeper than—a man's height," he gasped, "and I can't find it. It's gone!" he whined, as he watched the grey slime slither through his fingers. The temptation was too great. Derval had no doubt she would regret it but she could not resist it. Leif, in his anxiety for the gold cross, had momentarily forgotten about her. There he knelt at the edge of the pit, one hand held aloft, dripping with slime, the other resting on the slippery edge.

"Why don't you go in and search for it, you big ugly pig!" she shouted, throwing all her weight behind a jab of her foot into Leif's broad bottom. The result was immediate and spectacular. Leif shot forward and flopped face-down into the mess. There was a mighty splash as his huge frame ploughed into the slime. He choked and coughed, fighting desperately to right himself. His face was a horrendous sight as all manner of slop dribbled down his cheeks. It was a sight that Derval would never forget. She turned towards the street and ran. Behind her she could hear a terrible commotion.

"Get me out of here," Leif was spluttering, choking on the slime he had swallowed.

"Ah! My dress. My beautiful wedding dress!" Helga was shrieking. "It is ruined. What will I do, Solveig?" she cried, showing the great blotches of filth that had been splashed on the dress.

"Never mind the cursed dress!" Leif gasped. "Get me out of here!" Solveig looked from the distraught Helga to the choking Leif. There was only one thing she could do. She broke into hysterical laughter. The sight of the two women—one sobbing, one laughing—enraged Leif even more and he floundered about furiously. "You stupid,

stupid women! Send for Toren!" he gasped, spraying filthy liquid all about him as he flailed the surface in an effort to remain upright. "And look!" he screamed hoarsely, "that—little brat is running away! Stop her!"

Derval was well away at this stage. She hitched up her dress and tore down the street, not knowing, not caring, where she was going. She had to get away from Leif. If ever he caught her again, he would kill her. Of that she was sure. Weaving her way through the busy street and dodging the many dogs that snapped at her heels, she heard Helga call her name but she didn't even stop to look back. A sharp pain in her side eventually forced her to stop and rest. Where to go, she wondered, fighting to get her breath back. The river. Maybe Eoin is still down there, somewhere. But where?

The music of a whistle reached her ears above the din of the town. Further down the street she could see a youth, a few years older than herself, seated against a wattle fence, playing a tin whistle. A travelling musician. Maybe he has seen Eoin, she thought. Her breathing had eased by now. She moved warily towards the youth. His clothing was tattered and mud-spattered. Derval addressed him nervously.

"Can you help me?" she asked in a halting voice. The youth seemed to ignore her, intent only on his playing. She raised her voice. "Have you seen a boy? About this height. With fair hair and—"

To her surprise the youth stopped playing and spoke to her in a friendly manner. "Seen a boy?" he laughed, "I haven't seen a thing since I was a babe in arms!"

"Oh you're blind?"

"Daithí Dall, that's me. Blind since I was a little child."

"So you're Irish," she exclaimed. "I-I'm sorry you're

blind," she added hastily.

"There's no need to be. I'm well used to it by now. I know my way around Dyfflin better than any sighted man. The sounds and the smells tell me a lot! I play my whistle and sing at the markets and the feasting houses. I make a living from it. 'Tisn't much of a living but I'm happy enough. Now, what about you? Daithí Dall can tell you are unhappy."

"My name is Derval and I'm looking for my brother Eoin. We were taken from Killadoo by the one-eyed Leif—"

"Oh that fellow! He's a bad one!"

"He's a big ugly pig and just now he's swimming around in a cesspit," Derval said through gritted teeth.

"In a cesspit. In a cesspit?" Daithí chortled, slapping his leg. "Who put him in there?"

"I did," Derval said, in a whisper, looking anxiously about her. "I-I pushed him in."

"You? *You* pushed him in?" Daithí shook with laughter as he hauled himself to his feet. "That is surely the funniest thing that has happened in Dyfflin this many a month! I must hear more. Daithí Dall will write a song about Leif in the cesspit and Dyfflin will ring with laughter. Come, Derval. You must tell me the whole story. I have a little house down at the Fish Shambles."

"Fish—shambles?"

"Yes. Down at the river where they sell the fish. You'll be safe there. Come." Daithí strode down the street with all the confidence of a sighted man. He hummed to himself as he went, chortling now and then and giving occasional little leaps in the air. "Leif in the cesspit! Hee! Hee! Hee!" He tootled on his whistle. "Hee! Hee! Hee!"

"No! Wait!" Daithí suddenly checked his stride. "We

must see this. There will never be another chance to see Leif in a cesspit."

"You mean...go back?" Derval stammered

"Don't worry. Daithí knows his way around Dyfflin. You'll be safe if you stay close to me." He began to pick his way back along the busy street towards Solveig's house. Derval followed him nervously.

☐

"Come on, Toren. Pull!" Leif bellowed. "Get me out of this cesspit before the whole of Dyfflin comes to see me. Pull, you fool!" Toren strained and pulled with all his might, much to the amusement of a small group of women who had been attracted by the hubbub. Nobody paid any attention to the two young people who watched from behind a woodpile.

"Isn't this worth seeing?" Daithí giggled. Derval nodded, still nervous but also marvelling at how Daithí could "see" the fun.

"I'm trying, Leif," Toren grunted, "but you're a big man and the cesspit is very slippery."

"I know it's slippery, fool!" Leif shouted. There was a titter of laughter from the women. Leif glared at them. "What are you all standing there for, laughing at a man's misfortune? Go home, all of you or else give Toren a hand."

He turned back to the struggling Toren. "Come on, man. One big pull!" Toren wrapped the rope several times about his waist, dug his heels behind a rock, gritted his teeth and pulled. Beads of sweat formed on his brow and slowly rolled down between the blood vessels that stood out on his forehead. "That's it!" Leif grunted in encouragement. "That's it!" He dug his boots into the toe-holds in the side of the cesspit and inched his way upward. "Pull, Toren, pull!" At last he emerged from the slime and flopped on his belly at the edge of the pit. Toren gave one last heave before he too collapsed from his efforts. Leif lay still for a few seconds, looking like a beached whale. The women gave a mocking cheer and whispered among themselves.

Derval cowered behind the woodpile and tugged anxiously at Daithí's sleeve. "We must go! If he sees me now..."

"In a moment. Let's hear what Leif has to say for himself."

Leif dragged himself to his knees. "Bah! You stupid old hags! Clear off, the lot of you or I'll have you thrown into the cesspit. See how you'd like that!"

"Does that include me, Leif?" Helga asked.

"Hah! You were more worried about that dress than you were about me. I've a good mind to call off the wedding!"

"Now! Now! My big bear. Don't be so angry!" Helga was in a better mood since Solveig had assured her that the dress could be cleaned in time. "You'll feel much better after a good wash."

"Wash? I've got more important things to do—"

"The most important thing you have to do," Helga broke in, "is to get rid of that awful smell that's coming from you!"

"Hmph! Maybe you're right." He turned to Toren, who sat against the wall of Solveig's house, recovering from his rescue efforts. "Toren, somewhere down in that cesspit is a gold cross wrapped in cloth. I want it back!" Toren raised his arms weakly in protest but Leif would not be interrupted. "I don't care if you have to empty the whole pit, but I must have that cross for the wedding tomorrow."

"But Leif," the weary Toren pleaded.

"I want it back!" Leif roared, "or I'll have your head! Get some men to help you, but find that cross! And as for that little brat of a girl who has brought me so much misery, I will search Dyfflin until I find her and teach her a lesson she'll never forget. After I've had a wash!" He brushed past the giggling women. "Out of my way, you worthless hags! Don't fail me, Toren," he called back to his exhausted comrade. "The cross. Before tomorrow!"

Daithí and Derval did not wait to see any more. They moved quickly away and Derval didn't dare to look back. She kept her eyes fixed on the blind music-boy as he darted through a maze of settlements on his way to the Fish Shambles.

11

The Fish Shambles

Bríd re-arranged Eoin's wet clothes in front of the fire. "Well, you've certainly had your share of adventure, Eoin!" she said, poking the fire into life. Sorcha and Olaf had sat cross-legged, listening enthralled to Eoin's story.

"We'll have to help you find your sister," Sorcha said, her brow furrowed with concern.

"And the gold cross," Olaf added.

"Gold cross?" a voice queried from the doorway. "Who's looking for gold crosses in Dyfflin?" The voice was that of a tall, angular youth, some years older than Olaf. He flashed a warm smile to the group seated at the fire, as he lowered a large sack from his shoulder to the floor.

"This is Sven, my other son," Bríd explained. "Sven, this is Eoin. He has had a bad time with Leif."

"Hmm. That fellow is up to his old tricks again, is he?"

"And Eoin's sister is still with Helga, who will soon be Leif's wife," Sorcha added, adopting a serious adult voice.

"Very soon," Sven agreed. "Tomorrow in fact."

"How do you know that, Sven?" his mother asked.

By way of answer Sven emptied the contents of his sack before them. An assortment of animal bones of all sizes tumbled out. "That's how I know! I was down at the Flesh Shambles and you should have seen all the sides of beef and pork that were being bought and prepared for the wedding feast. It was good news for me. I got these bones and horns very cheaply!"

Eoin was totally puzzled by the collection that lay at his feet. "What do you need all those bones and horns for?" he asked.

"For my work, Eoin," Sven replied boastfully. "I am a comb-maker, the best in Dyfflin, some would say!"

"Hmph! *Sven* would say!" Sorcha taunted.

"Listen, you!" Sven turned on his sister. "There are women in this town who will have their hair combed only with one of Sven's combs. Aye, and they come looking for my needles, pins and spoons too."

"That's enough, you two!" Bríd interrupted. "We have no time to be arguing over Sven's combs. We must help Eoin to find his sister and then rescue her."

Sven sat on the pile of bones and stroked his chin. "That won't be easy," he said. "That Leif fellow will keep his one eye on her—"

"I told you she's with Helga, not with Leif," Sorcha corrected him, full of self-importance. "It just shows. No one ever listens to me."

"With Helga?" Sven ignored his sister's last remark. "That might make things easier...if we knew where Helga lived."

"It's somewhere near the Cornmarket. That's all I remember," Eoin said.

"Well that's a start," Bríd announced, rising to her feet. "Sven and Olaf, go and see if you can find—"

"No," Eoin interrupted, "I must go too. Sven and Olaf will not recognise Derval."

"But will Helga not recognise you?" Bríd reminded him.

Eoin paraded before her, drawing a hood over his head. "Not in my Viking clothes!" he laughed.

"That's true," Bríd agreed. "Maybe it's better if Olaf and Eoin go. Two young boys will not attract much attention. But be careful! Don't do anything foolish. Just find out what's going on and come back here. Sven will help you then. Off you go and God go with you!" The two boys waved goodbye and Olaf led the way to the Cornmarket.

They avoided the streets and kept to narrow passageways through various settlements. The people they met were busy with their crafts or trades and paid little attention to two Norse boys wandering casually past their workplaces. Eoin was amazed at Olaf's knowledge of Dyfflin and indeed at his brazenness at crossing other people's property. Soon they reached a familiar building. "This is the Cornmarket, Eoin," Olaf whispered. "Do you remember Helga's house?"

Eoin pushed back his hood to get a better view of the place. He paced up and down to get his bearings. "There are so many houses," he said, "and they all look the same. I think we went down the hill towards the river."

They moved in that direction but Eoin suddenly froze when a voice called out, "That's him, that's the boy from Killadoo!"

Olaf grabbed Eoin's arm. "Run, Eoin, run. It must be one of Leif's men!"

They were about to dart back through the maze of settlements when another voice cried out, "No! Wait, boys, wait. We are friends."

Eoin turned towards the men, his face beaming with

delight and relief. "They're not Leif's men! They're from Killadoo!" he announced to Olaf. He recognised one of the men immediately. "You're the man we shouted at in the Cornmarket yesterday."

"'Tis myself!"

"We thought you didn't recognise us!"

"We knew what you were up to all right," the man laughed, "but we weren't going to interfere, not with the mad Leif around, and not here in Dyfflin!"

The second man looked around anxiously. "So you are free now?" he whispered. "Can you come with us?"

"Well, I'm free, thanks to Olaf here, but my sister isn't. We have to find her and the gold cross of Killadoo, if Leif hasn't melted it down by now."

"You'd better be careful then," the first man warned. "If Leif catches you a second time, he'll make no mistakes!"

"He thinks I'm slaving away on the high seas!" Eoin giggled.

The second man was still very edgy. He looked up and down the street as he spoke to Eoin. "The message we have for you is that two cartloads of wattles will be coming to Dyfflin in two days' time. That will be your chance to escape."

"The carts will be at the riverside gate collecting wine," the first man added. "You must be there before sunset."

"If we can find Derval by then," Eoin promised.

"It's your only chance. We must go now. Good luck to you." The second man hurried back to his cart.

"Thank you and safe journey!" Eoin called, as loudly as he dared, but both men had melted away in the crowded Cornmarket. Eoin turned to Olaf. "What do we do now?" he asked.

"We still have to find Helga's house," Olaf reminded

him. "You said it was—" Their attention was distracted by a commotion further up the street. A group of people, laughing and jeering, was making its way towards them. "Probably a juggler or a clown of some sort," Olaf suggested.

As the cheering band drew nearer, however, Eoin realised to his horror what the source of the crowd's amusement was. It was a wet, bedraggled and foul-smelling Leif! The crowd teased him.

"Ha, Leif! Finally met your match!"

"Phew, what a smell, Leif. Is that a special perfume for your wedding?"

Leif put his head down and barged through them. "Out of my way, fools. The next one that opens his mouth..."

"Tell us about the bees, Leif!" a voice interrupted, and the whole crowd exploded in laughter.

Olaf and Eoin stood at the fringe of the crowd, enjoying the scene. Eoin made sure he was wearing his hood.

"Hee! Hee!" Olaf giggled. "Poor Leif! He looks such a mess!"

"But the bees, Olaf. How could they know about the bees?"

The man beside Eoin turned to him. "Have you not heard, boy? It's all over Dyfflin. How this little girl pushed Leif into a beehive and now she throws a gold cross that he captured into a cesspit...and she shoves him into the cesspit as well—"

"Into a cesspit? Leif?" Olaf and Eoin looked at each other and roared with laughter.

"'Tis true!" the man continued. "Daithí Dall is singing the story all over Dyfflin!"

"Daithí Dall?" Eoin queried.

"He's a blind musician," Olaf explained. "Daithí knows everything that goes on in Dyfflin. Why didn't I think of it before now?"

"Think of what?"

"Daithí. He'll know where to find Derval! Come on. Daithí lives down near the Fish Shambles. If we can find him we'll find Derval!"

They let the taunting crowd pass by and once again Olaf led the way in and out through the settlements. The Fish Shambles was a noisy, busy place where the fish merchants called out their wares in loud voices. As the two boys moved through the Shambles, they became aware that there was an unusual excitement in the air. Suddenly a voice called out above the others. "Hey, Daithí, tell us the story about Leif! All Dyfflin seems to know about it."

"Except us here at the Fish Shambles!" a second voice added.

The two boys looked at each other and moved to the centre of the Shambles. There, perched on an upturned fish-basket, sat a smiling youth, fingering a tin whistle. The fish merchants slowly gathered around the youth and encouraged him to sing.

"Come on, Daithí. I'm tired of carting fish around all morning. Sing us the song about Leif!"

"I'm not sure if I should!" Daithí laughed. "If Leif hears of my singing, 'tis me he'll be looking for and not a little girl!"

"Oh come on, Daithí! Sing for your friends."

"Well all right," Daithí relented, "but it's not finished yet because the story isn't finished!" He tootled a brief tune on his whistle and began to sing.

I tell the story of Leif leath-shúil
A warrior giant was he
Everyone obeyed his rule
On land and on the sea

All across this quiet land
He spread terror, he spread grief
And no one dared raise a hand
Against the mighty Leif

And then one day in Killadoo
In search of precious gold
Leif at last met his match
In an Irish warrior bold

Who was this brave warrior?
Well now it must be told
'Twas no gallant Irish soldier
But a girl twelve summers old!

Daithí's audience exploded into raucous laughter as he continued.

First she pushed him in the beehive
And covered him with sores
Then she pushed him in the cesspit
And you should have heard his roars!

Daithí concluded with a bow to his audience, who cheered and clapped loudly before returning to their stalls. Eoin could wait no longer. He called Daithí.

"Who is that?" Daithí asked. "A strange voice."

"My name is Eoin. I'm looking…"

Daithí leaped up and offered his hand to Eoin. "Come. Away from here, boy!" He led Eoin with Olaf following, away from the Fish Shambles. "You said your name was Eoin, so you're looking for Derval?"

"Yes. How did you know?"

Daithí placed his finger over his lips and stooped to enter a small dark house. A voice called nervously from within. "Who's there?"

"Don't be afraid, Derval," Daithí answered. "It's just Daithí, with some friends!"

"Derval!" Eoin exclaimed, throwing his arms about his sister.

"Oh, Eoin," Derval sobbed. "I thought I'd…never see you…again. How did you escape?"

"I jumped from the ship and Olaf here fished me out of the river, didn't you, Olaf?"

"You could say that," Olaf laughed. "The biggest catch I ever had."

"Olaf?" Derval shrank away from her brother. "But he's…"

"He's my friend, Derval," Eoin reassured her. "He saved my life. His mother is Bríd and she's been very kind to me."

"And now that we've found you, you must come to our house," Olaf added.

"But Daithí…" Derval began.

"Daithí will be all right," the blind youth assured her. "You go with the boys to Olaf's house. At least you'll be properly fed there. You won't have to live on Daithí's scraps!"

"And I nearly forgot, Derval," Eoin broke in excitedly, "we met the man from Killadoo—you remember? We shouted to him when Leif was bringing us to Helga's house and he told us there will be two carts from Killadoo at the riverside in two days' time."

"So all you have to do is hide in our house till then and—" Olaf began.

"But we can't leave without the gold cross!" Derval cried.

"Yes, we heard what you did with the gold cross," Eoin laughed, "and with Leif. I wish I had been there to see him in the cesspit!"

"But the cross!" Derval insisted.

"It will take ages to find it in the cesspit," Olaf explained, "and by then you'll be gone back to Killadoo."

"That's what I'm trying to tell you," Derval cried in exasperation. "The cross is not in the cesspit!"

"Not in the cesspit?" Eoin spluttered. "But if it's not there, where is it? What did you throw in the cesspit? And why?"

"One question at a time, Eoin!" Derval laughed. "It's very simple. That first night in Leif's house, I removed the cross from under his head when he was asleep. I had to tickle his nose to get him to move his head! And I had to put something in its place so I wrapped an old bone in the cloth and put it under his head. Unfortunately he began to stir so I panicked and hid the cross in the thatch of the roof!"

"And it's still there?" Olaf asked.

"As far as I know!"

"But what did you throw in the cesspit?" Eoin asked, shaking his head in disbelief.

"Leif's stale rye bread! I couldn't eat it last night but I wrapped it in cloth and kept it in case I grew really hungry!"

The three boys were stunned into silence for a moment before Olaf broke into laughter. "Oh Derval, you're far too clever for Leif and for all of us!"

"If only Leif knew where the cross really is!" Eoin added.

"Hee! Hee! Hee! What a joke!" Daithí giggled. "I'll have to add another verse or two to my song."

Derval's expression grew serious. "We must find a way of getting the cross back. But I don't know how. There's that savage dog of Leif's guarding the house."

"And tomorrow the wedding feast will be held there," Eoin added. "We'd never be able to get the cross back then!"

Olaf stroked his chin. "Maybe! Maybe we could! Maybe the wedding feast is just what we need."

"What do you mean?" Derval and Eoin said together.

"I'm just thinking of something. First let's get back to my house to work out a plan. Daithí, will you come too?"

Daithí shrugged his shoulders. "Alas, poor Daithí must try to earn a living singing his songs in the marketplace. But I'll keep my ears open for news of Leif! And maybe I'll go around to the wedding tomorrow to entertain the guests!"

"Good!" Olaf said. "Maybe we will see you there."

They parted company at the Fish Shambles. "Be careful, my friends," Daithí warned and in a moment he was gone from them. He was lost in the bustle of the town but as they headed back to Olaf's house the three companions could still hear Daithí's whistle above the noise of Dyfflin.

12

Council of War

A huge bonfire blazed outside Leif's house. Each time a log was tossed on to it, a shower of sparks shot through the billowing smoke. "That's it! Pile up the wood there," Leif ordered the two men who were tending the fire. He paced up and down like a caged animal, ignoring the music of Daithí Dall and the blind boy's appeal for money. Finally an angry voice interrupted his thoughts.

"Hey Leif! What are you trying to do? Burn down the town of Dyfflin?" It was Leif's neighbour, Erik.

"Don't annoy me, Erik," he snapped. "I need a good fire to roast the meat for my wedding guests. I tell you," he added boastfully, "Dyfflin will never see a feast like it!"

Erik was not impressed. "Dyfflin might not be around to see it, if that fire spreads," he warned. "The sparks are already landing on my roof!"

"Then you'd better catch them first," Leif mocked. "Can't you let a man enjoy his wedding?" he called, adding beneath his breath, "Interfering old fool."

Both men were suddenly distracted by the arrival of a very excited and very filthy Toren.

Daithí stopped playing his whistle. He giggled to himself as he strained to hear what would happen next.

"Leif, Leif, look!" Toren called, brandishing something in his right hand.

"Ah, Toren, you bring good news at last," Leif answered, rubbing his hands with glee.

"Yes," Toren announced breathlessly. "The gold cross, we found it in the cesspit!"

☐

Bríd shook her head in amazement as she listened to Derval's story. "'Tis no wonder you're the talk of Dyfflin, a ghrá," she said. "What do you think of her, Sorcha?"

"I've never heard of anyone who would cross Leif's path—never mind push him into a cesspit," Sorcha laughed. Derval slowly pounded a fist into an open palm to indicate her determination. "We still have to find a way of getting into Leif's house."

"The wedding feast will be held there tomorrow," Eoin added glumly. "We certainly couldn't get in then."

"Maybe we could—for that very reason!" The voice was that of Sven, who sat near the doorway for light as he scraped and shaped and cut a bone into an attractive comb. The others were silent, waiting for an explanation of his remark. Sven held the comb up to the sunlight, turned it in his fingers and then spoke as he made a slight adjustment to the comb. "It's really Olaf's idea. There will be a big crowd at the feast—if we can believe Leif—so no one will mind two girls selling Dyfflin's finest combs, made by Dyfflin's finest craftsman!" He bowed to his audience and held the finished comb up for their admiration.

"What do you mean—two girls?" Sorcha asked.

"You and Derval."

"But that would be too dangerous," Sorcha pleaded. "Leif would recognise Derval."

"Not if she were Sorcha's blind sister—and well covered up! Sorcha could do all the talking. She's good at that!" Sven wagged a mocking finger at his sister.

"Hmph! And where would Dyfflin's finest craftsman be?—home by the fire?"

"No," Sven replied calmly. "I would be up on Leif's roof—with Eoin."

"On the roof?"

"Yes. Look! The cross is hidden in the thatch, right? Only Derval knows where. So she stands under the place where she hid the cross and Eoin and I cut through the thatch and find the cross!"

Bríd was clearly unhappy with Sven's plan. "It's too risky, Sven. You will surely be noticed?"

"We will wait until dark. By then they will all be too busy drinking and feasting to notice us. And anyway, Olaf—"

"—will be keeping watch," his younger brother sighed.

"That's a very important job," Sven assured him.

"It's not exciting enough," Olaf complained.

"There's another problem, Sven," Eoin said. "Leif's guard dog, Wolf—he'd attack you if you even looked at him!"

There was silence. This was an unexpected obstacle. Sven had not known of Leif's dog.

Suddenly a solution came from an unexpected source. "Maybe I can help," Bríd suggested. "I know a thing or two about sleeping potions. Remember the potion I made for you, Sorcha, when you had the fever? I made it from berries we gathered in the wood. Now if I were to make that potion and cook some meat in it—that meat might make Wolf feel like a good sleep!"

Derval clapped her hands in delight. "That's a great idea, Bríd! Can you make the potion in time?"

"Of course. I'll go out to the wood at first light tomorrow." Bríd beamed with pride at her important role in the plan. "All this excitement is making me feel young again! Are you sure you don't want me to go with you tomorrow. I could be a big help—"

"N-no thanks, Mother," Sven interrupted. "Just stay here and—and say a prayer that all goes well!" He winked at the others.

"Yes," Olaf said, "and make that potion as strong as you can. From what Eoin tells me, this dog of Leif's is very like his owner—savage and wild!"

"And unlike his owner," Eoin laughed, "he has two eyes!"

"And an awful lot of teeth!" Derval added. The sound of Daithí's whistle interrupted their laughter. Bríd called out in welcome to Daithí, who was glad to come indoors. "Oooh!" he shivered. "There's a wind blowing out there that would play Daithí's whistle on its own!"

"What's the news, Daithí?" Derval asked.

"News?" His face glowed, as the fire brought heat back to his body and the memory of what he had witnessed came back to him. "Such news I have! You should have been there, Derval, and all of you."

"Tell us, Daithí."

"Well, Leif is in trouble with his neighbours. He's in danger of burning down Dyfflin. He has great fires burning to roast the meat for his wedding feast and his neighbours are all complaining that the wind will fan the fires and set their houses alight. That was bad enough but—" Daithí began to giggle uncontrollably.

"Come on, Daithí, tell us," Derval pleaded.

"Toren came along with the gold cross, or what he thought was the gold cross."

The children smiled knowingly.

"Poor old Toren," Daithí continued. "I can still smell him. And then Leif had to peel away this smelly cloth to find—"

"A piece of stale rye bread!" the children chorused, and broke into open laughter. Daithí was disappointed that the others knew this already, but gleefully went on with his story.

"Leif almost exploded," Daithí went on. He mimicked Leif's voice. "'Is this your idea of a joke, Toren?'"

The children cheered. Derval put on a furious face and joined in the mimicry. "'Stupid old ox,'" she boomed.

Daithí nodded. "And then Toren said, 'But we emptied the whole cesspit, Leif.'"

Tears of laughter welled up in the children's eyes.

"Poor Toren," Eoin whooped. "I feel so sorry for him. Leif treats him so badly. What other news do you have, Daithí?"

"Just that I never heard so many strangers in Dyfflin— all here for Leif's wedding."

"I didn't think he would have that many friends," Derval remarked.

"Most of them are Helga's friends—and such tongues they speak. They say the waterside is full of ships, from the north and the south lands. But they are a mean lot. Not one of them had a penny for Daithí!"

The laughter had subsided now and for a few moments there was silence as the children thought of the task that lay before them.

"You'd better keep yourself well covered up tomorrow,

Derval," Olaf warned. "If Leif recognises you, he'll roast you alive on the spit!"

"Ah—so you are going to the wedding?" Daithí asked.

"Well, we haven't been invited," Derval sniggered, "but we couldn't leave Dyfflin without paying Leif just one more visit!"

"Aha! Tomorrow will be an exciting day in Dyfflin," Daithí cried. "Daithí will be there too. I hope that when they have some wine in their bellies, those strangers will be more generous to poor Daithí. If not, I hope they get what they deserve!"

"What do you mean, Daithí?" Olaf asked.

"There's a rumour that there may be other 'visitors' to Dyfflin one of these days—Irish raiders! They might even attack tomorrow!" Daithí said with some excitement.

"I hope they wait until we get the cross back!" Derval remarked anxiously.

Sven was busily cutting another comb. He looked out at the darkening sky as leaden clouds banked to the west. "We could have quite a storm tomorrow too, by the looks of things!" he mused. "One way or another I don't think Leif is ever going to forget his wedding day!"

13

The Wedding

Sven's weather forecast was accurate. A violent storm broke out during the night. The wind whipped through the crevices in the wattle walls and caused the rain to sheer off the thatch in a wild cascade. Neither that nor the frequent thunder cracks woke the children however. It was only when Bríd returned from an early morning excursion to the woods that they stirred themselves.

"What a day!" Bríd muttered as she shed her dripping cloak and poked the embers of the fire into life. "Are you sure it's safe for you to go out at all, children? 'Tis as black as night and the rain would go through a person."

"It's just what we need," Sven said, peering through the gloom. "That rain will keep people indoors and the darkness will give cover to myself and Eoin when we're up on Leif's roof!" Bríd soon had the fire crackling beneath a pot of stew, which with generous helpings of her delicious bread gave the children a warm and nourishing start to the day.

The morning dragged by. Bríd concentrated on her potion and when she was happy with its strength she took a large lump of gristle and dropped it into the brew. Derval and Sorcha worked on Derval's disguise while

Sven fashioned a comb or sharpened his knives. Eoin fidgeted restlessly as he watched Olaf race straws on the rivulets of rain that streamed across the floor of the house. Olaf invited him to take part in the straw-racing but Eoin's mind was on other things. They were about to embark on a very dangerous adventure. One mistake and they would all be in trouble. Knowing Leif's mood at the time, "trouble" would certainly mean slavery, maybe even death. He shivered uneasily. He was sitting by a blazing fire so he knew it was not the miserable weather that caused him to shiver.

"Now, here's a present for Leif's dog," Bríd announced at last. "He'll be no trouble to you after eating that!" She wrapped the gristle in broad dock leaves and then in cloth and handed it to Eoin.

"Thanks, Bríd," Eoin said, feeling the warmth of the bundle as he stuffed it inside his tunic. "You've been a great help."

"Come on, girls," Sven called impatiently, "we haven't all day!"

"We're ready!" Sorcha announced. "Well, what do you think of my Viking sister?" she asked, parading the hooded Derval before them.

"Very good!" Eoin exclaimed, "I wouldn't know it was my sister. It is Derval, isn't it?" he joked, peering at the dark hood. Closer inspection showed that Sorcha had darkened Derval's face and hair with dye.

Derval did not respond to her brother's jibe. "She's blind and dumb, remember?" said Sorcha, "so I'll do all the talking for the two of us!"

"No trouble to you," Sven remarked. "Here, take these combs with you."

"Hmph! Not that anyone will buy them!"

"Hush, you two!" Bríd interrupted. "Leave the bickering aside for this day at least. Be careful now and God go with you!" She embraced each one of them in turn.

"Don't worry, Bríd!" Derval chirped. "We'll be back by nightfall—with the gold cross this time!"

Although it was only mid-afternoon, the dark and heavy clouds seemed to sit on the roof tops of Dyfflin, creating an eerie night atmosphere in the town. The rain still came sheeting down and the wind tore at the cloaks of the six shadowy figures as they darted through the sodden deserted streets of Dyfflin. The business of the town had come to a standstill. Anyone who was not at Leif's wedding was at home, huddled by a fire. The wedding guests crowded uncomfortably into Leif's house. The plan had been to let them wander around the settlement but the weather had ruined that. The guests jostled with each other for space to eat and talk.

"Hey Leif! How can you live in a town like Dyfflin?" an irate voice called out. "It never stops raining!"

"There are worse places, my friend," Leif growled, eyeing the man cautiously. He did not recognise him. A friend or relation of Helga's, probably. A fool!

"I can't imagine worse places," the man persisted. "Look, there are rivers running through your house! My feet are soaking and my wife's dress is ruined!"

"It's a little storm," Leif snapped. "Look. There's plenty to eat and drink. Enjoy yourself and stop complaining!"

"I'll say this for you, Leif. You know how to organise a wedding feast, but you and Helga will have to come and visit us in the south lands. There, at least, you don't have to splash around in your own house!"

Leif's simmering anger was about to boil over but fortunately for the guest, Helga intervened. "Ah there he

is! My big bear of a husband! Look what Lars the
woodcarver gave us for a wedding present!" She handed
Leif a finely carved wooden ornament which bore a face
on each side. "What is it, a two-headed monster?" Leif
grunted.

"You could say that!" Helga laughed. "It's supposed to
be you!"

"Me! That ugly pair? They're not even well carved.
Wait till I see Lars. I'll carve him up!"

"Poor old Leif!" Helga purred, putting her arms about
her husband. "Can't ever take a joke against himself."

"Joke! I've had enough 'jokes.' The whole town is
laughing at me because I was pushed into the cesspit by
that little brat!"

"Well it *was* funny, even if it meant I never got my
gold cross as a wedding gift."

"Don't worry, I haven't given up hope of getting it
back!" Leif growled.

"Come!" Helga said. "Let's have more wine. Nothing
else must spoil our wedding feast."

□

The six young people advanced cautiously towards Leif's
house. It wasn't easy to be cautious. They slipped and
slithered over the log street and constantly had to leap
over torrents of water which zigzagged crazily down the
slope. "What a day!" Sorcha muttered. "It's so dark. It's
more like night!"

"All the better for us," Sven hissed.

"Where's that guard dog?"

"Maybe he's inside the house," Eoin suggested, but a
vicious low snarl came in reply. "Spoke too soon! There

he is at the door, friendly as ever!"

Sven motioned to the others to stay in hiding while he advanced towards the dog. "Nice dog!" he called softly. "Look what I've got, Wolf. Eat that up!" He tossed the ball of gristle to the crouching dog, who snatched it in his powerful jaws and chomped viciously at it before swallowing it with relish. "That's a good boy," Sven said, retreating to his companions. They waited and watched.

"I wonder if Leif ever feeds him," Eoin said.

"Probably not, knowing Leif," Olaf replied.

"I wish he'd hurry up and fall asleep," Derval whispered through chattering teeth. "I'm getting soaked."

"Shush, Derval," Sorcha snapped. "You're supposed to be dumb, remember!"

After what seemed an age, the dog curled up in a sleeping position. Sven called to him but there was no response. "Well done, mother!" he whispered. "Now girls, in you go—and good luck!"

"It may take some time for me to find the exact spot where I hid the gold cross," Derval reminded the boys.

"So wait until you hear me call out 'Only one comb left! Who will buy my last comb?'" Sorcha added.

"All right. But be as quick as you can. We don't want to be up on that roof very long." Sven looked around. "Where's Daithí Dall?" he asked.

"He's already gone in," Olaf replied.

"Come, Derval," Sorcha called. "No more talking from you. You're blind and dumb. Take my hand."

"Good luck," Eoin called after them.

The two girls stepped over the sleeping dog and were faced with a wall of bodies as the guests, growing increasingly noisy and boisterous, fought their way to and from the wine and meat tables. "There's hardly room to move," Sorcha whispered. "Just nudge me where you want to go, Derval." Taking Derval in tow, she burrowed her way through the heaving mass and began to call out, "Combs for sale! Dyfflin's finest combs! Would you like a comb, lady? Combs for sale!"

☐

"Olaf, you stay in this shelter here and keep a sharp eye out," Sven commanded his brother. "If there's danger, whistle!"

"What danger could there be on a day like this?" Olaf complained. "Why can't I come with you?"

"Because we'd only be in each other's way," Sven said, placing his hand on Olaf's shoulder. "Keeping watch is important."

Sven crept away with Eoin to the side of Leif's house and in the shelter of a tall fence, he gave Eoin a leg up onto the roof. He then levered himself up by gaining toe-holds in the fence. They clambered across the roof, lying flat both to avoid being seen and to get a good grip on the slippery thatch. "This thatch is so wet," Eoin whispered. "Will it hold us up at all?"

"I hope so, otherwise we might be dropping in as uninvited guests!" Sven laughed. He handed a knife to Eoin. The sharp blade glinted in the rain. "Maybe we should spread our weight out. I'll go over the roof-ridge to the other side. Make a little peep-hole with that knife and see what's going on!" Sven slid over the roof-ridge while Eoin began hacking carefully through the thatch. Suddenly he paused. "Sven, did you hear a strange noise just now?"

"There are lots of strange noises from that lot down

there."

"No it came from behind me!"

"The storm?"

"No it wasn't that kind of noise."

"Well, I heard nothing. Now, cut away and tell me what you can see!"

☐

Inside the house it became more and more difficult for the two girls to move and for Sorcha to make herself heard. Suddenly they came face to face with Daithí Dall. "Oh Daithí," Sorcha cried. "Am I glad to see a friendly face! I haven't sold one comb! Not that that matters much."

"I know what you mean," Daithí replied. "This lot are either too drunk or too mean to part with a few pence for poor Daithí!"

"Sorcha! Sorcha!"

"Hush, Derval, you're supposed—"

"I know, but it's Leif!" Derval whispered in desperation. "He's right under where I hid the cross and he has passed out! He's snoring as if he'll never wake up!" Sorcha looked in horror at the giant figure sprawled out across two stools, snoring loudly. "How are we ever going to move that?" Sorcha cried.

"Leave that to me," Daithí said. "Just lead me to Helga!" Sorcha took Daithí's hand and fought her way to where Helga stood. Daithí tootled on his whistle. "A wedding is not a wedding until husband and wife dance together to Daithí Dall's music!" he called loudly.

Helga looked at Daithí and from him to the snoring Leif. "You're right!" she announced. "The big bear has had too much wine. Imagine falling asleep at your own wedding! I'll soon fix that!" She took the bowl nearest to her and sloshed its contents across Leif's face. "Come on, big bear! It's time to dance!" she shouted. "Come, dance with Helga!" Leif staggered to his feet, spluttering and cursing. The guests in the vicinity of Helga laughed heartily and cleared a small space where she and Leif could dance.

"Don't want to dance! Want to sleep! Go away!" Leif muttered.

Helga held on to the tottering giant and ignored his remarks. "That's it! Just put one foot in front of the other!" she coaxed. As the pair lumbered around, Derval studied the roof thatch closely, edged forward, then sideways and then stood very still.

"You're sure?" Sorcha whispered. Derval nodded. "Right! Here goes!" Sorcha drew a deep breath, looked towards the roof and shouted above the din, "*Only one comb left! Who will buy my last comb?*"

14

Attack!

Outside on the roof, Sven and Eoin clung on to the thatch in the face of even stronger wind and rain. They burrowed their numb hands under the top layer of thatch in an effort to work some warmth back into them. They had also to contend with the choking smoke that swirled in every direction from the smoke-hole. With great difficulty each boy had carved a peep-hole at one end of the roof so that between them they could see most of what was going on below.

When at last the code words came from Sorcha they strained furiously to see where the girls were. "Quickly," Sven called. "Over this end, Eoin!" Eoin scrambled across the roof, slithering downwards as he went. He looked through Sven's peep-hole and could see Derval a short distance away. "You'll have to guide me," Sven whispered, edging along to where he thought Derval stood.

Eoin placed one eye over the peep-hole and watched Sven's movements with the other. "Over another bit," he called, motioning Sven with one hand while he clung desperately to the soggy thatch with the other. "Now, down a little. Down! There! Start cutting!" He wriggled his way over beside Sven, who had begun hacking at the thatch. Sven worked furiously and with a lot less care than when he had carved the first peep-hole. He couldn't afford to be careful any longer; time was against him. The two boys huddled over the jagged hole that grew in the thatch.

"This thatch is hard to cut!" Sven grunted. "So wet and so thick. The edge has gone off my knife."

"Let me try," Eoin suggested. He knelt over the hole, took his knife in both hands, plunged it deep into the thatch and sawed the knife back towards himself. Sven propped his body against Eoin's to prevent him slipping. "I see what you mean!" Eoin panted. "I hope Derval is right. I can't..." Suddenly the knife scraped against metal. "That must be it!" Eoin cried. "I'll cut around it. See if you can loosen it."

Sven poked his freezing fingers into the thatch until they clasped an arm of the cross. "I've got it! It's coming!" He tugged at the cross, gritting his teeth fiercely. Eoin hacked around the area where the cross lay until finally it came free in Sven's hand. Eoin uncovered the cross and gave a cry of delight when he saw the glint of gold. Both boys collapsed exhausted across the hole in the thatch. It was an unguarded moment. Their combined weight pressed on the weakened roof and before they realised it the thatch began to sag and sway. A beam beneath them cracked loudly and in a moment the roof collapsed, sending the two bodies crashing, arms and legs flailing, on to the crowd below.

Such was the press of bodies on the floor beneath that the boys' fall was both shortened and softened. There were screams of terror and confusion as the two bodies landed with a thump on the scattering crowd. It was Eoin's misfortune that he landed on Leif and bowled him over on to the muddy floor. Sven literally fell into the arms of another brawny Norseman.

When it transpired that this was not a mass attack and that there were only two "invaders" the confusion died down quickly. There were moments of strange silence as Leif raised himself from the floor and slowly drew himself to his full height, rubbing a sleeve across his mud-spattered face. "Who? What?" he spluttered. He looked up at the gaping hole in the roof where by now the rain was pouring in. His gaze travelled downward to the two drenched youths who cowered before him. He realised that in the mêlée his eye-patch had been pushed upward, exposing an ugly socket where once there had been an eye. This combined with the boiling rage in his good eye made Leif an awesome sight as he advanced towards the frightened pair. Even some of the guests retreated before him.

"Who are you two?" he bellowed, adjusting his eye-patch and peering closely at the youths. "Who? Wait! I know you!" he shook a threatening finger at Eoin. "You're one of those brats who caused me all the trouble over that gold cross!" Sven instinctively slid the hand that still held the cross deep into his tunic. "You and that sister of yours who made me the laughing stock of Dyfflin! And now you wreck my house and my wedding feast!" He looked again in disbelief at the hole in the roof and raised his arm above Eoin as if to crush him with one blow.

Derval could take no more. "No!" she screamed, bursting through the startled onlookers to throw her arms protectively around her brother.

No one was more amazed by this intrusion than Leif. He paused, arm in mid-air, then slowly lowered it as a wicked smile crossed his face. "Aha!" he growled. "Aha!"

He tore the hood roughly from Derval's head. "I thought so! It's the other brat!" Leif danced a little jig of delight. He forgot about his wedding, his guests (many of whom were by now drifting away in disgust and discomfort), his ruined roof. He was talking aloud to himself. "I told you Leif would have his revenge in the end! I've waited to get my hands on you two!" He took a firm grip on Eoin and Derval. "When I think of all the trouble you have caused me. Well, this time there will be no mistakes. This time, Leif will have the last laugh! I'll put you both in chains and I'll personally see you off on a ship to some—"

"But Leif," Helga protested, "you promised me that girl would be mine."

"Well I'm breaking my promise!" Leif snapped. "I don't trust her. I want her away from here, out of this country forever!" He turned to his two prisoners. "How does that sound to you, brats?" he leered.

"Big ugly pig!" Derval spat the words at him defiantly.

Leif only laughed at her and tightened his grip on both of them. "Toren!" he bellowed. "Where are you, Toren?" A muffled reply came from the other side of the house. "I want this pair tied up in chains and...wait a minute! Wait a minute!"

In all the excitement of the capture, the really important thing was only slowly dawning on Leif. He turned back to Eoin and Derval and to Sven, whom he had ignored up to now. "Just what were you brats up to? Why would you come back to Leif's wedding once you had escaped from me? Eh?" He twisted Derval's ear. "There must be something here that you wanted? Maybe a gold cross? That's it! You came back for that gold cross!" he announced triumphantly. "Well, where is it?" he snarled.

Sven knew that he would have to make a move. Leif's

attention was less closely focused on him than on Eoin and Derval. He sidled as near as he could to Sorcha and, as Leif glared at Derval, awaiting an answer, Sven slid the cross to his sister and motioned to her to make a run for it.

Unfortunately for Sorcha, the glint of gold in the firelight caught Leif's eye and he pounced on her in a flash. "Well what have we here?" he crowed. "Another of these brats! How many of you are there? Come on! Hand it over before I—"

Leif was never to finish that sentence. For the second time in a short while, there was consternation at Leif's feast as, amid screams and whoops of surprise from the guests, a band of warriors burst through the doorway, while others leaped through the hole in the roof. This was no accidental intrusion by young boys. This was a planned raid by a band of Irish warriors, intent on revenge for some of Leif's attacks on settlements outside Dyfflin. The raiders caught Leif and his followers totally by surprise. "Toren!" Leif screamed. "My sword! I'll teach those Irish a lesson! Where are my guards? Toren!"

The wedding guests were unprepared for battle and could offer little resistance. Their screams, however, had raised the alarm and soon armed Norsemen arrived to do battle with the raiders. Someone tossed a sword to Leif, who charged like an enraged bull into the thick of the clash.

No one bothered with the children any more. Sven and Sorcha dived to the floor and began crawling towards the wattle wall. "Have you got the cross?" Sven cried.

"Yes. But where are Eoin and Derval?"

"They're following us!" Sven kicked furiously at the wall until he had burst a hole big enough for them to crawl through. Behind them there were loud screams as a raider went crashing into the fire, scattering blazing timber in all directions. The children crawled along the wall of Leif's plot, skirting the battle, until they reached a narrow lane at the back of the plot. They looked back briefly. An unnatural brightness came over the scene. It was not a lightening of the storm however. The orange glow told them that Leif's house had gone up in flames.

"Serves him right!" Derval smiled.

"Come on, we're not safe yet!" Sven called. "We must get home!"

"What about Olaf?" Sorcha asked.

"He would have seen this coming!" Sven replied. "He's well gone. Probably home before us!" They were about to run when they heard the familiar toot of Daithí Dall's whistle. "Wait for Daithí! This is no place to be making music!"

"Take my hand!" Sorcha called. "We'll get you out of here."

Sorcha and Sven, with Daithí in tow, ran pell-mell down the lane, across a street and through a maze of plots. Eoin and Derval stumbled along, glad to follow the others. The noise of battle faded but they could see a glow in the sky when they paused for a breather. Derval suddenly burst into laughter. "What's so funny?" the others chorused.

"Nothing much," Derval giggled. "It's just that when we were crawling out of Leif's house, I caught a glimpse of Wolf. There he was, murder and mayhem all around him, still fast asleep!" The laughter of the five echoed across the empty streets of Dyfflin as they headed for the safety of Bríd's house.

15

The Feast

It was a very relieved Bríd who welcomed the exhausted and bedraggled group back to her house. She hugged each of them in turn and looked anxiously around. "Olaf!" she cried, "where's Olaf?"

"Isn't he home?" Sven asked, "we thought—"

Bríd began to sob quietly. "My baby. Please do not let anything happen to my baby!"

Derval put her arm around Bríd. "He'll be all right, you'll see," she said softly. "He wasn't with us so he wasn't involved. He's probably just lying low until all the fighting is over. He'll be home soon. I know!"

"I hope you're right!" Bríd nodded. "He's a smart boy—but he's still a boy. Anyway," she said, lifting her voice, "I want to hear every detail of what happened. Gather round the fire. There's hot milk for you all."

They seated themselves around a blazing fire and gulped the milk, enjoying the inner warmth it brought. Bríd smiled and waited patiently. "Well," Derval sighed at last, leaning back on her hands, "we did it!"

"Yayyy!" the others chorused.

Bríd clapped her hands with glee. "You did it? You got the gold cross back? May I see it, please?" she asked excitedly.

Sorcha withdrew the cross from the fold of her dress and handed it to her mother. The firelight made the precious stones in the centre of the cross sparkle and threw the reflection from the golden arms of the cross all around the room.

"It's beautiful!" Bríd whispered, drawing in a long breath. "Beautiful!" She blessed herself with the cross. "May it bring a blessing on this house. No wonder you wouldn't leave Dyfflin without it!" She passed the cross around for each of the young people to appreciate the craft that went into its making.

"Poor old Leif!" Sorcha laughed, as she passed the cross to Daithí. "He'll never forget his wedding day!"

"He'll never forget Eoin and Derval," Daithí added. "They'll be singing about you both in Dyfflin for many years to come."

"We couldn't have done anything without you, our friends," Eoin said.

"Shhh!" Sven called suddenly. They listened and froze. Strange grunting and scuffling sounds came from outside the house. Could it be Leif? The young people exchanged nervous glances. Sven crept towards the door. The noises grew nearer. Sven cautiously peered out and then suddenly turned around with a broad smile on his face. "It's Olaf!" he cried, throwing the door wide open. "You gave us quite a fright, Olaf. What on earth have you got there?"

Olaf stumbled through the door. "Is anybody hungry?" he asked. "There's a present from Leif outside!" He fell into his mother's welcoming arms as the others rushed to see Leif's present.

"It's a pig!" Derval cried "A roast pig! But how—"

"Thanks a lot for waiting for me," the exhausted Olaf panted. "I had to carry and drag that pig through the back lanes of Dyfflin all by myself! Where did you all go anyway? Did you not hear my warning whistles?"

"I'm afraid not," Sven laughed. "We had already dropped in to Leif's feast! Then when the raiders came, our only escape was down the back way. Now tell us what happened to you!"

"I managed to stay hidden until after the raid," Olaf said, still cradled in his mother's arms.

"You mean the raid is over already?" Eoin asked in surprise.

"The Irish don't wait around very long after these raids," Sven said.

"What about Leif?" Derval asked. "Is he...?" She had good reason to wish the worst of fates on Leif, but something inside her wanted him to escape.

"Poor old Leif," Olaf laughed. "He's sitting there in the ruins of his house, muttering to himself!"

"In the ruins?" Sorcha asked.

"Yes, his house was burned down, and several others too! His wedding guests have all scattered. There was lots of food around and no one to eat it."

"Not even Wolf!" Eoin laughed. "He's probably still asleep, thanks to Bríd's potion."

"So I helped myself to a pig," Olaf concluded. "I can tell you it's not easy to carry a roast pig through the flooded streets of Dyfflin!"

"I told you you were doing important work," Sven said, ruffling his brother's matted hair. "See! You end up providing a feast for all of us!" Daithí struck up a tune on his whistle. "Let's celebrate the return of the gold cross of Killadoo!" he suggested.

"And Leif's wedding!" Eoin teased.

"If only he knew we were feasting on his roast pig!"

said Derval.

They feasted and joked long into the night as each of the six recalled the details of Leif's wedding for Bríd, who laughed herself to tears.

□

The next morning was in complete contrast to the previous day. The storm had cleared overnight and a bright and warming sun rose over Dyfflin, lifting hearts and encouraging people to come out of the houses in which the storm had imprisoned them. Once again, Dyfflin was bathed in light and noise as work and trade got under way. In every home and workplace the conversation was about the raid and the wedding.

Daithí Dall stirred himself before the others had woken fully. "I'll slip away and see what's happening around the town," he said. "Hee! Hee! That sounds good—I'll see what's happening!" he repeated, mocking himself. "Never mind! A blind boy can see a lot! Derval and Eoin, meet me at my house before the sun starts to set. It's near to where the carts will be!" He said goodbye to Bríd and her family before darting off, tootling the merriest of tunes on his whistle.

"That boy would cheer the heaviest heart!" said Bríd, watching him from her doorway.

The morning crawled along. For Derval and Eoin the excitement and anxiety they felt about their trip back to Killadoo that evening was tinged with sadness at parting from their friends. It was agreed that Olaf would bring them to Daithí's house, since he had not been seen with them at the wedding feast. The time came for them to leave.

"Thank you for all your help," Derval said, her voice choking with sadness at parting from Bríd and her family. "We couldn't have done it without you!"

"God bless you," Bríd said, wiping a tear from her eye. "You were only with us a few days but even so it seems you are part of our family!"

"We are—and we always will be," Derval said. "I hope we meet again some time."

"And we'll tell our friends in Killadoo that not everyone in Dyfflin is a wild Norseman!" Eoin added.

"Well, you are not back in Killadoo yet, so be careful of that wild Norseman," Bríd laughed. "Here's something for the journey." She handed them a bundle each. "Some of that bread you like so much and some pig-meat! We seem to have a lot of pig-meat!" she laughed. "And...and God go with ye!" She turned away quickly but Derval and Eoin followed her and hugged her warmly.

"Here's something to remind you of Dyfflin's finest comb-maker," Sven said. "A comb each for you and your mother, Derval, and two fine bone toggles for you and your father, Eoin!"

"T-thanks," Derval stammered, not knowing where to look.

"All I have to offer is a hug," said Sorcha. She embraced Eoin and Derval in turn.

There was an awkward silence before Bríd coughed and said hoarsely from a darkened corner, "So, let you go, or you'll miss the carts!" Derval and Eoin muttered a goodbye, waved and slipped away with Olaf, not daring to look back...

16

The Warm South Lands

The three children kept to the back lanes, avoiding the sunlit open spaces. Derval and Eoin were silent as Olaf led them across the town that was by now becoming familiar to them. Once or twice a group of Norse people passed by, chattering loudly and gesturing wildly. When that happened, Olaf dropped to his knees and motioned to the others to do likewise. He then picked up a handful of pebbles and began playing a game, shooting a large pebble at a smaller one with his thumb. Who would pay any heed to a group of Dyfflin children, playing a game of stones?

At last they reached Daithí's house, but as yet there was no sign of the blind boy. The time seemed to pass quickly now as Derval watched the sun's path anxiously. "Where can he be?" Eoin asked, peering up and down the street.

"Don't worry," Olaf said. "Daithí knows his way around Dyfflin. He's just making sure there's no sign of trouble."

As if in reply, there came the familiar toot on the whistle from up the street. Daithí dashed in, breathless.

"We were getting worried, Daithí," said a relieved Derval. "Is there trouble?"

"The only trouble is getting through the crowds down at the riverside," Daithí gasped. "Most of them seem to be Leif's wedding guests—and what they haven't got to say about Leif and his wedding!" he chortled, as his breathing returned to normal.

"Any sign of Leif?" Derval asked.

"No. He's probably hiding till all his guests have gone!"

"Let's hope he stays in hiding till we have gone," Eoin said. "If he came across us again, there would be no questions asked. He'd just slice us in two with that big sword of his!"

"Come on," Derval urged. "It's time to go. We must find those carts from Killadoo quickly!"

They said goodbye to Olaf. "Good luck with your fishing!" Eoin said.

"I'll never catch a bigger one than you!" Olaf laughed and, with a cheery wave, he was gone.

They headed for the town gateway by the river embankment. Daithí listened carefully before crossing the open space towards the gateway. Derval and Eoin followed, trying to appear casual, while a fearful heart beat rapidly within each of them. Suddenly Daithí froze, cupping a hand to his ear. Derval looked around frantically.

"What is it, Daithí? There's nothing..."

"It's Leif. He's coming this way!"

They were caught now surely, in an open space with their enemy advancing towards them. They looked to the fringe of the crowd but could see no sign of Leif. Nevertheless, they trusted Daithí's "seeing ear." Eoin looked around in desperation. Just to their right he noticed an upturned coracle. It was their only hope. "Quick, Daithí! In here!" he whispered, grabbing the boy's arm.

The three crawled under the coracle, cramping their

bodies to allow the boat to sit naturally on the ground. They held their breath as footsteps approached and a familiar booming, angry voice came into earshot. "Come on, woman! What's keeping you?"

Faintly they heard Helga's reply. "I'm coming! I'm coming! Not everyone can keep up with a big bear like you, especially an angry big bear!"

"Hmph!" Leif snorted, and to the consternation of the trio inside he plopped his huge body down on the upturned boat, causing it to sag severely in the middle as the light fabric strained and began to rip under his enormous weight.

"And why shouldn't I be angry?" Leif snapped, as he rested uneasily on the boat. "Just look at all the trouble I've had since I met those two brats at the monastery. I've had nothing but bad luck with that gold cross. I tell you if I got within a sword's length of them this minute I'd...What? What was that?" He stood up abruptly, looking very puzzled.

"What was what?" an equally puzzled Helga asked.

"I thought I heard someone laughing, children laughing."

"Really, Leif. The sooner you leave Dyfflin the better. You imagine those children laughing at you all the time. You have nightmares about them!"

"Why shouldn't I have nightmares? My wedding feast ruined, my house burned down by those invaders, nearly all my possessions destroyed. Nightmares? Life is a nightmare in this miserable place!"

"Well not for much longer," Helga said. "There's Ivor's ship delaying for us, bound for the warm south lands."

"Well, what are we waiting for then?"

"We're waiting for Toren, who has to carry our

belongings, since you were too lazy to do so."

Leif shaded his eyes from the sun and looked back towards the town to see the laden figure of Toren lumbering towards him. "Come on, you old ox!" he shouted. "You're getting very slow!"

"Maybe if you carried some things it would help!" Helga said drily.

"That's it! Blame Leif! Everything is Leif's fault! Bah! I should have stayed in the homeland!" Leif kicked at the boat to express his annoyance. Inside the three children clung together desperately, fearing that at any moment a stronger kick would bring Leif's foot crashing through the skin of the boat.

"Indeed! If you had stayed in the Norselands you would have starved and," Helga's voice softened, "you would never have met Helga! Come on, you grumpy old bear, or Ivor will sail without us. Come Toren! It's not much further."

"I'm glad to hear that!" Toren gasped. At last the footsteps and the booming voice of Leif began to recede. The children went limp and lay in a heap under the boat, exhausted with anxiety and fear.

Eoin scarcely had the energy to prise up the edge of the coracle. He was just in time to see Toren disappear through the gateway in the river embankment—the same gateway through which Leif had led him on their way to the waterfront. "They're gone!" he cried. The three struggled out from under the boat and were glad to stretch themselves and breathe in fresh air again.

Derval looked at the sun. It was sitting on the western embankment. "Quickly!" she cried. "We've got to hurry." They raced towards the western gateway and were relieved to see two carts drawn up near the gate. Two men were struggling to load wine barrels on to one of the carts. Eoin recognised one of them as the man who had spoken to him a few days earlier.

They reached the carts, breathless. "We thought you weren't coming," the man from Killadoo said. "Another little while and we'd have been gone. Hop in quickly behind those wine barrels. There's no need for you to hide. I hear you have driven Leif from Dyfflin," he laughed.

Derval turned to Daithí Dall. "Won't you come with us to Killadoo?" she asked. "You'd like it there—and the people would like you."

Daithí paused before shaking his head. "Daithí must stay where there are people—lots of people—to hear his songs!" he sighed. "And the people of Dyfflin will hear the story of Derval and Eoin for many a day to come!"

Derval hugged him. "We'll miss you, music-boy—and thank you for all your help!"

Eoin shook Daithí's hand and he climbed aboard the cart with his sister. The men were anxious to leave. "Goodbye!" they called to Daithí, who replied with a tune on his whistle. Their last view of Dyfflin was of a ragged boy playing a cheery tune on his whistle as he danced and skipped his way towards the Fish Shambles. They crouched low behind the barrels as the carts trundled through the western gate.

Freedom! Derval thought, as she clasped the gold cross inside her dress—just to make sure...

17

Killadoo

As Dyfflin receded behind them, the children came out of hiding and perched side by side on a barrel. They watched the setting sun through long shadows across the smoky noisy town. How good it was to be in the countryside again—to see the woods waving on each side and to hear the familiar call of birds on the evening air. As they weaved and bobbed to the movement of the cart they smiled at each other. Neither Eoin nor Derval spoke. There was no need to speak. Each had memories of the last few crowded days. Once Eoin tugged Derval's sleeve and pointed to the wood. In the fading light they could just discern two pigs rooting among the leaves in the undergrowth. Freedom! They laughed aloud and remembered the food that Bríd had provided for the journey. They ate with relish and thought of their good friends in Dyfflin. Derval sleepily hummed a tune as two tired bodies propped each other up on top of the wine barrel.

They were suddenly woken from their drowsy state by the sweetest music they could imagine—the monastery bell of Killadoo! In the distance they could see the round tower illuminated in the darkening evening by a large bonfire. This was no fire of Norse destruction. This was a fire of welcome. "We're home, Eoin, we're home!" Derval said softly, gripping her brother's hand.

As they came within hailing distance of the monastery, the children could see two figures running excitedly towards the carts. Even in the dark of evening they could recognise the athletic stride of their father and the slower but graceful movement of their mother. With a whoop of joy they jumped from the cart and raced to meet their parents, leaping into their arms with cries of delight. All four clung tearfully to each other. Their mother would not let go of the children but clasped them to her, gently murmuring their names and uttering little prayers of thanksgiving.

Eventually a procession of monks and other families who lived beside the monastery came to greet the children and one big happy group made its way, laughing and talking excitedly, back to the safety of the monastery. Above all the din, the bell rang ceaselessly. "Will someone tell Brother Cormac to stop ringing that bell?" Brother Killian called. "If he doesn't, he'll have the Norsemen back here again!"

The group gathered round the bonfire. "Well you won't have Leif back—that's for sure!" Derval laughed.

"Indeed! We heard you drove the poor man out of Dyfflin!" Killian said, "and later we want to hear the whole story around this fire. Killadoo needs a good laugh! But first...the cross?" His red cheeks glowed with excitement in the firelight.

"The cross?" Derval replied, giving Eoin's foot a gentle tap with her toe.

"Yes, yes, the gold cross of Killadoo," Killian said impatiently.

"Oh, the gold cross," Derval repeated looking extremely puzzled. "The gold cross...Have you got it, Eoin?"

"No," the equally puzzled Eoin replied, "I thought you had it!" They stared blankly at each other and then turned to Killian before exploding into laughter.

"Well you're a right pair of rascals and no mistake," Killian sighed. "My poor old heart nearly stopped there. You had me fooled!"

Derval took out the cross and handed it to Killian, who held it aloft for all to see. There were murmurs of delight from all sides at the sheer beauty of the craftsman's work. Killian raised his hand to silence the crowd. "That we should have this beautiful cross here this evening is due totally to the bravery of two young people, Derval and Eoin!" His voice was drowned by a mighty cheer from the crowd. "And now," he said quietly, "we will put the cross back where it belongs." He led the group into the little oratory, where he fixed the cross above a shrine. Prayers of thanksgiving were said. As Derval stood holding her mother's hand, looking up at the cross, the memories of the previous days came flooding back to her. All the pain, all the loneliness, all the hurt—it had all been worthwhile just to see the gold cross of Killadoo restored to its rightful place.

A silence descended on the crowded oratory. Suddenly Brother Cormac tottered in and called aloud, "Have they gone? The Norsemen? Someone said I scared them away with my bell..."

"They've gone all right, Cormac," Killian replied. "And we're going out to celebrate by the bonfire—and to hear the full story of the adventures of the gold cross of Killadoo."